CRUEL
LOVE

CHECK OUT ALL THE BOOKS IN THE
NEW YORK TIMES BESTSELLING **PRIVATE**
AND **PRIVILEGE** SERIES BY KATE BRIAN

PRIVATE   PARADISE LOST

INVITATION ONLY   SUSPICION

UNTOUCHABLE   SCANDAL

CONFESSIONS   VANISHED

INNER CIRCLE   OMINOUS

LEGACY   VENGEANCE

AMBITION   LAST CHRISTMAS

REVELATION   THE BOOK OF SPELLS

PRIVILEGE

BEAUTIFUL DISASTER

PERFECT MISTAKE

SWEET DECEIT

PURE SIN

CRUEL LOVE

CRUEL LOVE

PRIVILEGE NOVEL

BY

KATE BRIAN

SIMON & SCHUSTER BOOKS FOR YOUNG READERS

New York   London   Toronto   Sydney

An imprint of Simon & Schuster Children's Publishing Division
1230 Avenue of the Americas, New York, New York 10020
This book is a work of fiction. Any references to historical events,
real people, or real locales are used fictitiously. Other names, characters,
places, and incidents are the product of the author's imagination,
and any resemblance to actual events or locales or persons,
living or dead, is entirely coincidental.
 is a trademark of
Simon & Schuster, Inc.
For information about special discounts for bulk purchases,
please contact Simon & Schuster Special Sales at 1-866-506-1949 or
business@simonandschuster.com.
The Simon & Schuster Speakers Bureau can bring authors to your live
event. For more information or to book an event, contact the
Simon & Schuster Speakers Bureau at 1-866-248-3049 or visit our
website at www.simonspeakers.com.

Produced by Alloy Entertainment
151 West 26th Street, New York, NY 10001

Book design by Andrea C. Uva
The text of this book was set in Adobe Garamond.
Manufactured in the United States of America
2 4 6 8 10 9 7 5 3 1

Library of Congress Control Number: 2011925963
ISBN 978-1-4424-0788-6
ISBN 978-1-4424-0789-3 (eBook)

FIRST
EDITION

For Lanie, from beginning to end

UNFAIR

All around Ariana Osgood, the sounds of the emergency room dimmed to a dull hum. The flashing red lights outside the thick-paned window faded in and out. An ancient coffee machine in the corner hissed as it gurgled hot brown liquid into a mug. A few droplets of fresh, red blood splattered the tiles as someone limped by. A child cried. A mother screamed. Someone, somewhere, begged for help. But Ariana was unaware. For her, time had stopped.

For her, there was nothing in the world but Reed Brennan.

She must die . . . she must die . . . she must die . . .

The mantra pounded at the base of her skull like a drumbeat, a call to arms, a battle march.

She must die . . . she must die . . . she must die . . .

Ariana focused on Reed's mouth. On her lips. The lying, back-stabbing, love-of-her-life-stealing lips, as they babbled away to a police officer. Spewing more lies, no doubt. Explaining things away.

Claiming innocence. Poor, poor Reed. Always, always, *always* the victim. Steadily, the mantra grew faster.

She must die . . . she must die . . . she must—

There was a slam over by the admittance desk and suddenly the world zipped back into focus. Noise and color and light and pain crashed in on Ariana from all sides.

". . . don't know what happened," Reed was saying. She hugged her scrawny arms around her scrawnier waist. "I thought she had a ride home. I was sure he was driving her home . . ."

A tear slipped from Reed's eye and she swiped it away. Ariana tilted her head. It was amazing, really, how unchanged the girl was. Same bland, shapeless clothes, except, oddly, her coat appeared to be a bland Kenneth Cole number rather than a bland Old Navy. Same dirt-brown hair. Same off-putting angular features. Same dull brown eyes. She wasn't as tall as Ariana remembered. Certainly not as strong. In fact, Ariana was quite certain that if she walked over there right now, wrapped her fingers around Reed's skinny neck and squeezed, she could have her dead within a minute.

She must die . . . she must die . . . she must die . . .

Ariana's fingers twitched at her sides. Her mouth began to water. This was it. Her opportunity. The moment she'd been anticipating for three long years. It would have been marvelous if she had been able to execute her original plan and shoved Reed off the roof of Billings House those many moons ago. It would have been dramatic and messy and best of all, done. But this . . . this would be so much more poetic. She would look Reed in the eyes as she died. Watch the light and the life go out of her. Feel her agony, her desperation, her fear. She would witness the very moment that Reed recognized it was over—that Ariana had won. That she had finally, finally won.

She must die . . . she must die . . . she must die . . .

"I should really call her roommate. She must be freaking out," Reed said.

She tugged a cell phone out of her pocket and began to turn. In half a second, she would be facing Ariana. Their eyes would meet. Ariana couldn't breathe.

"Ana. I need to talk to you."

Someone grabbed Ariana's arm. She looked up into the stricken, pale face of her soon-to-be-ex-boyfriend, Palmer Liriano. His green eyes were raw and his brown hair mussed, as if he'd run his hands over it and back a thousand times. Behind him, Soomie Ahn sobbed against Maria Stanzini's shoulder, her straight black hair sticking to the tears on her cheeks. Jasper Montgomery talked in low tones with Landon Jacobs and Adam Lazzerri, all of them looking fearful and gaunt. Tahira Al-Mahmood cried silently as her boyfriend, Rob Mellon, tried to console her. Everyone she knew was gathered around, looking out-of-place in their formalwear, elaborate hair, and carefully applied makeup as they whispered, blubbered, and prayed. Prayed for Lexa Greene, Ariana's best friend, who had tried to kill herself by jumping through the glass roof of the greenhouse at Maria's mansion.

And just like that, the drumbeat stopped. Ariana's world snapped back into focus. Her *real* world. The world in which she now lived.

One that didn't include Reed Brennan. One that *couldn't* include her. Reed turned toward Ariana, and Ariana buried her face in Palmer's chest. She took in a few hopelessly broken breaths, squeezed her eyes shut, and closed her hand around her forearm.

Get it under control, Ariana. Get it under control.

She gripped her own arm as hard as she could, her fingernails digging into the skin.

"Ana? Ana? Are you okay?"

Palmer's strong hands closed over her shoulders. He pushed her back slightly so he could look into her eyes. Ariana blinked up at him. In her peripheral vision, she saw that Reed was gone. Maybe outside to make her call. Maybe to the bathroom. Maybe back to the Georgetown campus, where Ariana knew she currently lived. Whatever the case, for the moment, the danger was over.

Slowly, Ariana began to breathe again.

She nodded shakily. "Sorry. I just . . . I got dizzy there for a second . . . thinking about all the . . . the blood," she improvised.

"Okay. You're all right now?" Palmer asked, his tone all business.

Ariana looked down at her arm. She was bleeding. Her fingernails had broken the skin. She covered up the wounds with her palm, trying not to wince, and nodded again.

"Anything new about Lexa?" she asked.

Palmer shook his head. "No." Keeping his hands on her shoulders, he ducked his chin to look her in the eye. "Ana, you've been spending more time with her than anyone. Did you have any idea that she was thinking about . . . about doing *this*?"

"No," Ariana said. "I mean, we all know she's been acting a little off lately, but . . ."

Lexa had been acting more than a little off. Ever since Ariana had murdered Kaitlynn Nottingham in front of Lexa, she hadn't been herself. She'd gone completely OCD and was prone to sudden, unexpected freak-outs and breakdowns. For the past few nights, Ariana had been feeding the girl Valium to help her sleep, and it seemed to have been working, but that evening Jasper had said something about knowing Ariana and Lexa's secret, and Lexa had assumed the worst—wrongly. Before Ariana could tell Lexa they were safe, Lexa came crashing through the glass ceiling.

"But if you knew something, you would have told someone, right?" Palmer demanded, his eyes intense. "You know you're supposed to tell someone? You're supposed to get the person help."

Ariana stared up at him, trying to process his words—his patronizing tone. "Palmer . . . if I'd thought Lexa was going to kill herself, of course I would have done something."

"I mean, you're supposed to be her best friend, right? You're supposed to know these things," Palmer's voice grew louder with each word. "Or maybe you guys weren't as close as you were always claiming to be."

Ariana's face was on fire. All her friends turned to stare.

"Palmer, please. Calm down. You're just upset," Ariana said.

"Of course I'm upset," Palmer said, bringing his fist to his mouth. "Lexa's in there clinging to life and you're telling me there was nothing you could do to stop it."

"Palmer, that's enough," Jasper said, putting a hand on Palmer's shoulder from behind. "This is not Ana's fault."

"Get off me, man," Palmer said, swiping Jasper's arm away and starting to pace like a rabid animal. "All I know is, Ana and Lexa have spent every minute of every hour together for the past two weeks. How many times have you broken dates with me because you just had to hang out with your BFF?" he said sarcastically. "Well you couldn't have been such great friends if you'd let her go off and do something like this!"

"Palmer, stop!" Maria gasped.

Suddenly, Palmer froze. He looked around at the gaping faces of his friends, as if realizing for the first time that they were there. Then he looked at Ariana. Her eyes burned with unshed tears and her chest heaved beneath her huge diamond necklace. Who the hell did he think he was? She was the one whose best friend was inches from death. He was supposed to be consoling her, not accusing her.

I should have broken up with you before the party, she thought, clenching her teeth. *I should have done it days ago.*

But she had been afraid. Afraid of losing her It-Girl status on the Atherton-Pryce Hall campus. So now, here she was, getting publicly berated on one of the worst nights of her life. One more nudge and she was going to lose it. She could feel it in her hot, trembling veins.

"Screw you, Palmer," Ariana said through her teeth.

His brow knit. "What?"

"We're over," she snapped.

Everyone stared at Palmer. Ariana could see all the hurt and pain and confusion whirling in his eyes and, for once, had absolutely no idea what he was going to do next. Suddenly, he grabbed his overcoat off his chair and stood up straight.

"Fine," he said. "If that's what you really want, then fine. We're broken up."

He gave her a sidelong glance and Ariana was certain there was something else he wanted to say, but he thought the better of it, cleared his throat, and walked out of the emergency room.

Ariana looked at Jasper, her true love, and just like that, the tears spilled over. He moved toward her like he was going to take her in his arms, but Maria and Soomie got there first. Which was just as well. No one knew that she and Jasper had been seeing each other behind Palmer's back, and now didn't seem like the right time to get into *that* drama.

"He doesn't really blame you," Soomie said, holding Ariana's hands as Maria brushed her hair back from her tear-stained face. "He's just freaking out like the rest of us."

"Yeah, but he's the only one who felt the need to go accusing Ana," Maria said sarcastically. "Men are bastards," she said under her breath.

Ariana rested her head on Maria's shoulder.

"You know this isn't your fault, right?" Soomie said, squeezing Ariana's hands. "None of us saw this coming. None of us."

Ariana nodded. "I know," she said, her voice thick.

But I should have. I should have seen what was happening, she thought. *And now Lexa's in there dying because of me.*

She glanced over at the police officers who had taken Reed

Brennan's statement about whatever she had been blubbering about. She breathed in and out, trying to get the tears under control. Trying to make sense of everything that had happened. How was it possible that the one person in the world she would have liked to see dead had just walked out the door, and the one person in the world she would have liked to see live was practically dead in the next room?

Sometimes, life was just so unfair.

COMFORTS

She must die . . . she must die . . . she must die . . .

Somewhere between the hospital and the front gates of the Atherton-Pryce Hall campus, the mantra started up again. Ariana stared out the window as headlights flashed by and tried as hard as she could to block it out. She sang songs in her mind, she recited all the states and their capitals, she tried to remember the first, middle, and last names of everyone in her class at Atherton-Pryce.

Nothing worked.

By the time the taxi she'd shared with Jasper, Tahira, and Rob pulled up in front of the looming towers of Privilege House, she was exhausted in body, mind, and soul.

"I wonder if everyone already knows," Tahira said, staring up at the windows as Rob paid the cab driver. "That is *not* a story I want to tell over and over again."

"I say we just ignore everyone," Rob said, squeezing her shoulder. "It's what we usually do anyway."

He and Tahira exchanged a weary smirk and together, they all exited the car. The night air was frigid and Ariana wrapped her arms around herself, wondering why she hadn't thought to wear a wrap over her gray gown. Jasper automatically put his arm around her and Ariana flinched. Rob and Tahira were right there. But then she remembered: She'd broken up with Palmer. She and Jasper could do whatever they wanted now.

"I need coffee," Tahira announced as they entered the lobby. Her shoulders were slumped, her usually perfectly applied makeup hadn't been retouched all night, and her strapless black dress was in desperate need of a pulling-up. But her appearance, for once, was clearly the last thing on her mind. "You guys wanna go sit in the café?"

Jasper let Ariana go and they exchanged a glance. "No thanks. I'm pretty exhausted," Ariana said. "I just want to go lie down and pretend this day never happened."

"Me as well," Jasper said, rubbing his forehead. "I could sleep until next Tuesday."

"Okay then." Tahira pulled Ariana into a hug. "She's going to be okay, you know."

"I hope so," she said flatly.

"She will. She's Lexa," Tahira said with a confident smile. "She's unstoppable."

Ariana ventured to smile, but she couldn't seem to make it happen. If the last couple of weeks had proved anything, it was that Lexa wasn't as strong a person as she'd once thought.

"See you in the morning," she said.

Rob lifted a hand to Jasper and Ariana as he put his other arm around Tahira. Together they headed for the café on the far side of the common room. Jasper slipped his hands into the pockets of his suit pants and half smiled.

"Shall we?"

He hit the up button on the elevator that served the girls' tower of the dorm. It pinged and the doors slid open. Together, they stepped inside. As soon as the doors closed, Ariana was in Jasper's arms. Neither of them said a word as the elevator zipped them to the top floor. Ariana simply breathed in his spicy, comforting scent.

The volume on the mantra dulled ever so slightly. Dulled to a slight thrum rather than a pounding beat.

She must die . . . she must die . . . she must die . . .

Upstairs, Jasper led Ariana back to her room. She paused for a moment at the threshold, looking around at the slight disarray left behind as she'd gotten ready for the fabulous formal Stone and Grave event they'd attended tonight. Tubes of mascara and lip gloss were still set up on her desk. The clutch purse she'd decided against sat at the foot of her bed, and a pair of black Christian Louboutins were upended near the closet. Ariana had agonized all day over which shoes to wear. Just thinking about it now—the awful shallowness of it all—made her want to throw the shoes out the window. Instead she kicked them into her closet, slammed the door, and went right for her dresser. She pulled an Atherton-Pryce Hall sweatshirt on over her head and unzipped her gown, letting it fall to the floor. Then she

shimmied into a pair of yoga pants and climbed into bed, her diamond necklace still sparkling around her neck. Jasper undressed down
to his T-shirt and pants and climbed in next to her. He put his arms
around her and Ariana rested her cheek on his chest. The mantra now
was barely audible.

She must die . . . she must die . . . she must—

"I still can't believe it," Jasper whispered, stroking Ariana's hair.
"Lexa Greene. She is the definition of having it all. I guess it just
proves that you never know what's going on inside people's minds."

Ariana squeezed her eyes closed. *I knew,* she thought. *I knew how
distraught she was. Palmer was right. I should have done something. I
should have known . . .*

"Can we talk about something else?" Ariana whispered. Her voice
was a mere squeak. She hated how weak and scared she sounded.

"Yes. Of course. Sorry." Jasper kissed the top of her head. Ariana
pressed her ear closer to his chest, listening to the comfortably rhythmic sound of his heartbeat. For the first time in an hour, her brain was
silent. "I do have a question for you, actually."

She tilted her head back so she could see his face. "Yeah?"

"Yes." He shifted slightly, crooking his free arm behind his head.
"Earlier tonight . . . what did you think I was going to tell you? What
was the secret you thought I'd found out?"

Ariana's heart thumped so hard she was sure it was going to stop
beating altogether. Suddenly terrifying images flashed through her
brain. Images of her shoving Jasper against a shelf-lined wall in the
potting shed. Of her holding a pair of rusty, dirty garden shears to

his neck. Of the fear in his eyes as he begged her to stop.

How the hell was she supposed to explain that? Ariana pressed her lips together and racked her brain. The "secret" Jasper had found out was that Briana Leigh Covington, the girl Ariana was currently pretending to be, had hooked up with a female professor at her old school. What other secrets could Briana Leigh have had? Secrets that might merit such a drastic reaction?

As she looked around her room, her eyes fell on a framed photo of the ranch house where Briana Leigh had grown up. Ariana remembered the last time she was there, and her encounters with Briana Leigh's rich, crotchety old grandmother. "I thought you'd found out that I bought my way into Atherton-Pryce," Ariana said, thinking quickly. "Lexa is the only person who knows, so when you said the two of us had been very naughty . . . I figured you'd found out about the bribe and that she was keeping the secret for me."

She paused and licked her lips. It was thin, she knew, but it was all she had.

"I didn't want the other members of Stone and Grave to find out, especially not the alumni, because even though I might have gotten in through a back-door deal, I've worked so hard since I've been here," she rambled. "I'd like to be judged on the basis of that, rather than the fact that my grandmother felt the need to grease the admissions board."

Jasper said nothing. Ariana picked a speck of lint off his T-shirt and crushed it between her thumb and forefinger. He wasn't buying it. She could feel it.

"I just want everyone to believe I deserve to be here," she said finally.

Because I do, she added. *After everything I've been through, I so, so deserve to be here.*

"Well, anyone can see that," Jasper said.

Ariana looked up at him, feeling a thrill down her back. "Really?"

"Are you joking? You ace all your classes, you were the star of our pledge class, you were here about five seconds before you made friends with Lexa's crowd." Jasper pulled a face and scoffed. "You deserve to be here more than anyone I know."

Ariana smiled and leaned in to kiss him. His hand went around the back of her neck and brought her in even closer. Ariana felt a stirring deep inside of her, but tamped it down. This was not the time to be getting physical. Not with Lexa in the hospital. She broke off the kiss and bit her lip.

"You know I never would have really hurt you, right?" she lied. She had been about to hurt him. She had been about to slaughter him, in fact. Anything to keep her secrets. It would have killed her to do it, but a girl on the run had to do what a girl on the run had to do. "I was just messing around."

"I know," Jasper said, cupping her shoulder with a grin. "Besides, I like a girl who can take care of herself. Less work for me."

Ariana rolled her eyes, but laughed.

"Remember the other day when I invited you to Thanksgiving at my house?" Jasper asked.

Ariana's heart fluttered. "Yeah."

"Well? The offer still stands and my parents would love to meet you," he said. "Have you thought any more about it?"

With everything that had gone on over the past few days, Ariana had completely forgotten about the invite. But after the awful drama of the night, running off to Louisiana with Jasper and putting Atherton-Pryce behind her for a few days seemed like a dream.

"I have and I'm in," Ariana replied. "I can't wait to meet your family."

Jasper grinned. "I'll book you a ticket in the morning."

Ariana smiled and settled in again, cuddling into the crook between his arm and his chest as she imagined a big, picturesque family Thanksgiving—something she hadn't experienced in years. She was more thankful for Jasper than for anything or anyone else in her life. If she had pulled a pair of garden shears on Palmer, he probably would have broken up with her in disgust and turned her in to the police for attempted assault, goody-goody that he was. Everything with him was black and white, but Jasper knew there were other shades to the world. As she inhaled the clean scent of his T-shirt it suddenly hit her full force that she could have lost him tonight. The horror of it crashed over her like a tidal wave, threatening to sweep her away and she found herself clinging to the front of his shirt.

Don't leave me, she thought. *Please don't ever, ever leave me.*

"Ana? Are you okay?" Jasper asked.

Ariana forced her fingers open and released his shirt. A little mound of white cotton stood up in the center of his chest.

"Can you just . . . stay with me? Until I fall asleep?" she asked.

"I was planning on staying the whole night," he replied.

He leaned down and kissed her ever so softly, and within minutes, Ariana had drifted off to sleep.

COME TOGETHER

Wearing her black Stone and Grave robe, Ariana stood at her designated place between Tahira and Landon. The cavelike room beneath the library where all official meetings took place was as still as night. Candles flickered along the stone walls, set in sconces and candelabras of various heights and sizes, but other than the occasional rustling of a bell sleeve, the room was eerily silent. Ariana stared at the empty spots on the opposite side of the circle. Lexa, the president, was missing, of course. But the spot next to her, usually occupied by Palmer, was empty as well, as was the spot next to April Coorigan, usually occupied by Lexa's boyfriend, Conrad Royce. No doubt they were both stationed dutifully at Lexa's bedside.

Lexa's current love and Lexa's ex were each claiming a proprietary spot in the vigil. Ariana wondered if anyone had picked a fight yet. She hoped that if they had, Conrad had given Palmer a sound pummeling.

Finally, April lifted the hood from her head, exposing her mass of red curls. "We are the Stone and Grave," she intoned.

"We are the Stone and Grave," the rest of the brotherhood replied.

"You may be seated," April said.

Robes swished and throats were cleared as the membership settled in on the cold stone floor. Ariana crossed her legs and sat up straight.

"I wonder what this is all about," Tahira whispered. "Are we setting up a service for Lexa or something?"

Ariana shrugged as April began to speak.

"I'm going to dispense with ceremony for the evening," she said clearly, her Irish brogue coming through. "We've all been through a lot in the last twenty-four hours, and we have some business to attend to, but first I wanted to give you all an update on our president."

Ariana shifted her legs as everyone around the circle adjusted and squirmed, exchanging nervous, scared glances.

"I spoke to Lexa's mother this afternoon and there was, unfortunately, no change," April said, blinking rapidly as if trying to hold back tears. Still, her voice came through crystal clear. "Lexa has been through three surgeries to stop some internal bleeding, and her body has suffered a lot of trauma. She's currently unconscious, but breathing on her own. They're not sure when . . . or even if . . . she's going to wake up."

"She's *going* to wake up," Soomie snapped, leaning forward. "Don't say that."

The membership froze. Rarely, if ever, had Soomie raised her voice—and definitely never at a Stone and Grave meeting. Ariana swallowed a hard, cold lump in her throat.

"I apologize, Sister Emma Woodhouse. I was merely repeating the facts as they were told to me," April said calmly.

"Well, it's crap." Soomie crossed her arms over her stomach and looked at the floor. "She's going to wake up. She's going to be fine."

April took a deep breath. "Is there anything else anyone would like to say? About Lexa or the situation or . . . anything?"

No one said a word.

"All right then," April continued, casting a wary glance at Soomie. "As the highest-ranking member of the order now present, it's my duty to enact the bylaws of our ancient brotherhood. Those bylaws state that if our president is incapacitated and unable to fulfill his or her duties, we are required to elect an interim president."

Soomie scoffed, rolled her eyes, but said nothing. Landon raised his hand.

"Yes, Brother Pip," April acknowledged with a nod.

"Wouldn't Palmer . . . I mean, Brother Starbuck just become president? Since he's the V.P.?"

"That *would* make life easier, but unfortunately, that's not the way it works," April replied.

"As far as I'm concerned, Brother Starbuck has no business acting as president anyway," Tahira grumbled.

A few people exchanged confused glances, but Ariana noted that those who had been present in the ER the night before turned to look at Ariana, their expressions grim.

"Seriously," Maria said, reaching back to quickly tie her long brown hair into a floppy bun. "The guy's a gargantuan asshole."

Ariana hid a smile behind her hand.

"Hey!" Landon protested.

Maria shot him a death glare from the other side of the circle. "An asshole who can't handle a crisis," she added. "Is that really the type of person we want running our chapter?"

"Look, the guy was freaking out, okay?" Landon said. "You can't hold it against him."

"Whatever," Soomie put in, rolling her eyes. "It doesn't matter anyway. Lexa's going to get better and she'll be back before we know it. Whoever gets elected will probably only be in office a couple of weeks."

Her assertion was met with complete quiet. Ariana glanced at Tahira and knew they were thinking the same thing—that everyone in the *room* was thinking the same thing—Soomie was in denial. Of course, no one had actually *seen* Lexa. No one knew firsthand how severe her injuries were. But anyone with a grasp on reality had to know that even if Lexa did get better, she wouldn't be back at school for a while, if at all.

"Maybe we should just take nominations," April said, looking around the circle. "Anyone?"

At that moment, Ariana's cell phone let out a loud ring. Tahira flinched and Ariana glanced around apologetically as she tried to fish the phone out of her back pocket.

"I'm sorry. I know we're supposed to turn them off. But I thought that, under the circumstances . . ."

Ariana slid the phone out and checked the screen. She had one new text message. Her heart rate sped up when she saw that it was from Conrad.

"It's from Brother Lear," Ariana said, her thumb quaking as she opened the text. She stared at the words for a moment, her mind going blank, her skull weightless.

"Well? What does it say?" Soomie demanded.

Ariana looked up. The flickering candlelight seemed to dim and brighten and dim and brighten. "Lexa's awake."

THE HONOR

The pink light of dawn was just warming the windowpanes of the ICU waiting area when Mrs. Greene finally emerged from Lexa's room. Ariana and her friends lifted their heads in unison, like some macabre ballet. In her rumpled green sweater set and gray pants, Lexa's mother looked exhausted, but also hopeful. The eyeliner around her eyes was smudged, and she wore no lipstick, but there was a small smile on her dry lips.

"Ana?" she said, lacing her fingers together. "Lexa is asking for you."

Ariana's heart skipped an excited beat as all eyes turned to her. It was all she could do to keep from shooting a triumphant glance in Palmer's direction. He'd already been here when Ariana and her friends had arrived, but had stayed seated in the corner, far away from the rest of the crowd. Over the past couple of hours he hadn't moved a muscle and hadn't uttered a single word to anyone.

Think our friendship is fake, huh? Ariana thought as she smoothed the front of her eyelet cashmere sweater. *Idiot.*

Jasper reached up and gave Ariana's hand a squeeze. She lifted her chin as she followed Lexa's mother down the hallway. This was an honor, being the first person summoned to Lexa's bedside, and she felt the import of it down to the tips of her toenails.

Ariana paused outside the door. She looked hesitantly at Lexa's mother. "Is she . . . I mean, is she . . . okay?"

There was no way she could ask what she really wanted to ask, which was how grotesque Lexa looked. She wanted to be prepared, but she was certain it would be impolite and unkind to press her mother for details.

"I won't lie, dear, it's a bit of a shock at first," Mrs. Greene said, reaching up to fiddle with her pearls. "But you get used to it."

Ariana nodded, placed her hand on the cold steel door handle, and walked inside. She half expected Lexa's mother to come with her, but the door closed slowly and quietly behind her. The moment Ariana saw Lexa she froze, realizing how stupid her question to Mrs. Greene had been. Nothing could have prepared her for this. Lexa was turned away from her, but Ariana could see that one side of Lexa's face was a huge purple bruise, so swollen Ariana could barely make out the slit of her eye. Angry black stitches clung to a huge gash along her cheekbone, and her battered face was covered with hundreds of tiny cuts.

Slowly, Lexa turned her head to face Ariana. The other side of her face looked relatively untouched except for a few red scratches. Her hair had been shaved back over her ear and a bandage was taped to her skull. Only one of her hands was visible—the one with all the IVs and monitors attached to it—and it lay limp atop the light blue hospital blanket.

"I know, right?" Lexa said, her voice scratchy. "I could have my own horror franchise."

Ariana managed a small laugh and took a tentative step toward her friend. "Are you in much pain? Do you need anything?"

Lexa closed her eyes briefly as she swallowed, as if the mere act took concentration. "No. I'm good. I'm so hopped up on painkillers I feel nothing."

Carefully, Ariana lowered herself onto the edge of the chair at Lexa's bedside. She felt as if touching or moving anything could set off an alarm.

"Ana, listen . . . I asked you to come in here because I wanted to tell you . . . I've decided I'm going to tell my parents about what happened with Lily."

Suddenly Ariana felt as if the floor had dropped out from under her. She reached out and grasped the cool metal safety rail around Lexa's bed as her vision darkened with gray spots.

"No," was all she could think to say.

"I have to, Ana," Lexa said, her voice sounding tinny and very far away. "It's going to be okay. It was all done in self-defense. I'm sure my father will make sure nothing happens to you. But I have to tell them. Clearly, I have to tell them," she added, looking down at her broken body. "I can't handle it anymore. You have to understand."

The temperature in the room seemed to grow warmer with each

passing moment. Ariana reached up and tugged at the collar of her sweater, trying to breathe. Trying to think. Trying to see past the gray spots. This could not happen. She could not let this happen. This would mean the end of everything.

And then she saw it. Sitting on a countertop on the opposite side of Lexa's bed. A silver tray lined with medical equipment. A pair of scissors. A roll of gauze. A scalpel. A syringe. Slowly, Ariana pushed herself to her feet and walked around the end of Lexa's bed.

"Do you want to talk to them with me?" Lexa asked, following Ariana with her eyes. "If we told them the story together . . . exactly how it happened . . . it might come out better."

Ariana glanced down at the tube running into Lexa's left arm. It was filled with dark red blood. She was receiving a transfusion even as they talked.

"Sure," she said, her voice flat. "Sure, I'll do it with you."

"Really?" Lexa's head lifted a centimeter from her pillow, then fell back again. Apparently just that effort was too much for her. She closed her eyes and breathed out through her mouth. "Thank you, Ana. I knew you'd understand."

Ariana tugged a pair of plastic gloves from a cardboard box on the counter and pulled them on, making sure not to snap the wrists. She lifted the syringe, keeping her back to Lexa. Slowly, she sucked a nice, big pocket of air into the syringe.

"Of course I understand. We can't have you trying to kill yourself again," Ariana said.

Lexa exhaled once more and tears seeped out from under her closed eyes. "I just . . . I couldn't see any other way out," she said. "That night I just . . . I couldn't imagine making my parents suffer through that scandal. Us possibly ending up in jail. Everything seemed so bleak. I just . . . I couldn't take it anymore."

"I understand," Ariana said calmly.

She turned around and used the very tip of the syringe to prick the tiny tube carrying the lifeblood into Lexa's vein. Then, ever so quickly, she pushed down on the plunger, emptying all the air into the tube.

Lexa's eyes opened, focusing on Ariana's face as Ariana dropped her hands down to her sides and behind her back, tucking the syringe out of view.

"Thank you, Ana. I don't know what I'd do without you."

Suddenly, Lexa's eyes went wide. Her mouth dropped open as she gasped out in pain. Her hand fluttered up from the mattress as if reaching for her chest, but there was no time. It sank back against the sheets again, and the line on her heart monitor went flat.

Quickly, Ariana returned the syringe to its proper place, ripped off the gloves, and shoved them into her pockets. Then she lunged for the door, as any surprised, panicked visitor might do under the circumstances. She was just reaching for the handle, when the door flew open, almost taking her down.

"What happened?" a male orderly shouted at her.

"I . . . I don't know," Ariana stuttered, backing herself against the wall as a crash cart came careening through. "She just . . . one second she was talking and then she gasped and closed her eyes and . . . is she going to be all right?"

"You need to go, Miss." A nurse placed her hands on Ariana's arms and shoved her out the door. Mrs. Greene was just stepping out of the elevator with a cup of coffee and nearly collided with Ariana. Her face went slack and the coffee hit the floor.

"Lexa?" she said tentatively. The she saw what was going on inside the room and screamed. "Lexa!"

Ariana's friends jumped up and gathered around the doorway of the waiting area, clinging to one another, straining to see what was going on. Jasper stepped forward and pulled Ariana back, away from the commotion.

"What happened?" Soomie asked tearfully. "Ana? What happened?"

Ariana swallowed hard. For the first time in the last several minutes the whole world was in sharp focus. She could see the freckles on Maria's face, the stubble on Palmer's chin, the striations in Tahira's lips. They all looked so frightened. So devastated. So sad.

And she had caused it. This time, it was all down to her.

But what was she supposed to do? She couldn't let Lexa spill all her secrets. The girl would have ruined everything. She would have trashed the life that Ariana had worked so tirelessly to build. If Kaitlynn's body were exhumed, it would be about five minutes before the authorities figured out she was actually an escaped convict, then another ten minutes before they realized that Briana Leigh Covington was actually Ariana Osgood. Ariana would have been back in jail before she could blink.

There was no way Ariana could let Lexa do that to her. If Lexa wanted to screw with her own life, that was her business, but Ariana would *not* let Lexa screw with hers. Not now. Not when she was so close to having every little thing she'd always wanted.

She must die . . . she must die . . . she must die . . .

Both Reed's and Lexa's faces swam in Ariana's vision. Her brain began to prickle and she closed her eyes. For a moment, they were the same person, Lexa's round chin, Reed's sharp cheekbones, Lexa's green eyes, Reed's split-ended hair.

"Ana?" Jasper was saying. "Ana? Are you all right? Do you need to sit down?"

Ariana shook her head. She took a deep breath and opened her eyes. "No," she said, her voice harsh. "No. I'm f—"

Suddenly, the tumult in Lexa's room died. Silence reigned. The heart monitor was turned off, quieting the incessant tone.

"No!" Lexa's mother screeched, clinging to the doorjamb as the doctor tried to reach for her. "Noooooooo!"

"Oh my God," Maria whispered.

Soomie buried her face in Adam's chest. Palmer let out a strangled cry. Conrad turned around and walked off by himself, his hands over his face. Ariana simply stared. Stared at the doctor's eyes as he gazed down at Lexa's grieving mother.

"I'm so sorry," he said quietly. "She's gone."

WHAT FRIENDS ARE FOR

"Soomie, you've been up all night. You have to try to get some sleep," Maria said soothingly. Ariana stood inside the doorway of Soomie's single dorm room—the room she'd had to herself ever since her roommate Brigit Rhygstead had died almost two months ago. She had never seen Soomie look quite so disheveled, quite so exhausted, quite so unfocused. She sat in the center of her bed, still wearing the same clothes she'd had on all night and day—skinny jeans, a chunky black cable knit sweater, and low-heeled black boots. The sweater was pulled down over her knees all the way to her ankles, and her knees were shoved up under her chin. She had her arms wrapped tightly around her legs as she rocked forward and back, staring down and to the right at the base of the wall next to her bed.

Ariana walked to Soomie's desk, put down the bag full of comfort foods she'd just acquired from the café and glanced at Maria. Maria's brown eyes were pained as she rubbed Soomie's back with her flat hand. "What's . . . going on?"

"She was awake." Soomie's voice was flat and toneless. "She was awake and she was going to be fine. She was awake and we were all going to get to see her."

"I know, Soom, but just because she'd woken up . . . that didn't mean she was completely healed," Maria said, leaning forward in Soomie's desk chair, angling toward the bed. "The doctors must have missed something."

Yeah, like a big, deadly air bubble in her vein, Ariana thought, watching Soomie closely. Her eyes were shot through with red and her nose was swollen. Her black hair hung in clumps around her shoulders and she kept tapping her fingers on her shins, like she was playing piano or hitting the keys on her BlackBerry.

"But she was awake, and I was going to get to see her," Soomie said. One tear dropped from her eye onto her knee.

Maria looked up at Ariana, her own face drawn and tired. It was amazing how grief seemed to age people. Just looking at Maria now, Ariana could perfectly imagine how she was going to look at thirty years old. Still pretty, but in a dulled way.

"She's been saying some variation of that, and only that, for the past half hour," Maria said, keeping her voice down.

Soomie's head snapped up. "Don't talk about me like I'm not even here!" she shouted.

Both Ariana and Maria jumped. Maria raised her hands and pushed her chair backward. "I'm sorry. I was starting to think you were going catatonic on us."

"Well, I'm not. I'm not crazy, okay? I'm not Lexa," Soomie snapped.

She shoved herself up from the bed and crossed over to the far wall. The school had long since removed Brigit's bed and her other furniture—a favor they hadn't yet granted Ariana, even though she'd been without a roommate since Halloween—so the wall was completely bare. Soomie let out a groan.

"I just don't get it," she said, whirling to face the others. "Lexa had never been depressed a day in her life. Why did she do it? What could have possibly happened that would make her kill herself? Why didn't she just *tell* us about it?"

"I don't know," Maria said quietly, slumping in her chair. "I guess we'll never know."

Ariana swallowed against her dry throat. "She *had* been acting a little strange lately, though," she said, knowing full well that the girl had been acting just this side of bonkers. She felt as if she should try to come up with some reasonable explanation for all of this—some way to make Soomie feel better. "Was there . . . I mean, could there be a history of mental illness in her family or something?"

"The Greenes? Please," Soomie scoffed, crossing her arms over her chest. "They're like America's most perfect family."

"Well, except for the infidelity," Maria pointed out. "And the constant power struggles."

"And the ego-mongering, and the mind games," Ariana added. "They do have a thing for extreme behavior."

Soomie looked at them like they were losing IQ points by the moment. "They're in politics! Hello?"

"Okay. Fair point," Maria said. She pressed her slim hands against her thighs as she stood and crossed to the picture window looking out over the icy waters of the Potomac. "I just can't believe she's actually gone. Lexa Greene. Dead. We're never going to see Lexa again."

Ariana and Soomie walked over slowly and stood at Maria's side. In the distance, a wide-winged gull swooped over the water, dipping and diving, before finally perching on a low, flat rock on the far bank. Quietly, Ariana's stomach grumbled. She wondered how long they were going to stand here in silent contemplation. There was a ham-and-cheese croissant in that bag across the room, calling her name. She glanced sidelong at Maria and Soomie and told herself to suck it up. These were her friends, after all. The only ones she had left, aside from Jasper and possibly Tahira.

"What was the last thing she said to you, Ana?" Soomie asked, her voice hushed but hopeful.

Ariana thought back, wondering if she should lie. But what could be more perfectly poetic than Lexa's actual final words?

"She said, 'What would I do without you?'"

Soomie's eyes brimmed with tears. Maria covered her mouth with one hand. Ariana let out a melancholic sigh.

"I guess now we're all going to have to figure out what *we're* going to do without *her*," she said.

Soomie started to cry in earnest and Maria turned toward her, wrapping her up in her arms.

"I don't think I can do this, you guys," Soomie sputtered, her whole body shaking. "I don't think I can take any more of this. Another funeral, another wake, seeing her parents . . ."

"Shhhh." Maria stroked her hair. Ariana put one arm around Soomie's shoulders and rested her cheek against the top of her head. Before long, Maria was crying, too, and soon Ariana felt tears streaming down her cheeks as well as they all grieved for their fallen friend.

FIGMENTS

As the white casket was slowly, painstakingly lowered into the ground, Mrs. Greene fell to her knees in the dirt. The sound that escaped her throat was like something from another, tortured reality—loud and shrill and throaty at once. A tall woman who could only have been her sister crouched next to her in her high heels, trying in vain to haul her back up. A pair of photographers swooped in for a better shot, but Senator Greene turned his wide shoulders toward them, barring their way. Throughout the funeral service at the church, the paparazzi had managed to be respectful, but apparently this unbridled show of emotion was more than they could resist.

"Lexa! Lexa!" Mrs. Greene wailed, reaching toward the massive hole in front of her.

Ariana finally turned her head, pressing her face into Jasper's shoulder. He held her tightly and whispered into her hair, but she couldn't make out the words. Next to her, Maria sobbed uncontrollably. Here and there throughout the large crowd, sorrowful moans and strangled cries rose up toward the bright blue sky, as several of the mourners found themselves unequal to the task of holding it all inside.

"Can we get out of here?" Ariana whimpered.

"Of course," Jasper said.

The people on the outskirts started to break away. Ariana looked around and saw that many of her classmates were exchanging hesitant glances, unsure of what to do. Across the way, April held hands with Kassie Sharpe. Conrad stared at the casket, a rose in one hand, stock-still and bleary-eyed. Tahira and Rob clung to each other as Tahira tried to get control of her breathing. Behind her, Reed Brennan slipped a pair of dark sunglasses over her eyes and turned toward the waiting line of cars.

Ariana's heart stopped. Reed? No. No. No. What was she doing here? She took a step toward the casket—toward Reed—and almost tripped as Jasper started to tug her the other way.

"Ana? Where are you—?"

Reed could *not* be here. She had no right. No place. Ariana's fingers curled into fists as her vision started to prickle over with gray spots. Suddenly, the drumbeat that had been silent for the past two days thrummed to life inside her skull.

She must die . . . she must die . . . she must die . . .

Then Reed turned and looked right at Ariana. And it wasn't Reed at all. This girl's face was wider, her nose broader, and in a black Calvin Klein she was certainly dressed better. Slowly, Ariana's eyes cleared and her body temperature began to cool. The drumbeat quieted to a dull thud.

"Ana? Are you okay?" Jasper asked.

Ariana turned, the wind tossing her hair in front of her face. She saw that a few of their other friends had gathered to wait for her. Adam was there with Quinn and Jessica, two of the sophomores who used to wait on Lexa hand and foot. Soomie, however, was nowhere to be found. Ariana could scarcely believe that her friend would miss the funeral. Ariana thought back to the other day—Soomie rocking back and forth on her dorm room bed—and felt a thump of foreboding. Her friend's absence could only mean that something was very, very wrong.

"Yeah . . . yeah, I'm . . ." She glanced over her shoulder, but the Reed-like girl was gone. Palmer was walking off in the opposite direction between his parents, his head bowed. Conrad still stood over the grave, staring into it, one red rose hanging limply from his fingers. "Let's just go."

She looped her arm around Jasper's and Maria took her other hand. Together they began to walk slowly toward the parking lot. Tahira and Rob caught up with them as they made their way over the clipped grass, skirting ancient headstones and stepping around a recently covered grave.

"When's everybody leaving for Thanksgiving?" Maria asked, sniffling.

"My parents are flying here and we're all going to my cousins' house," Rob said, holding Tahira tight to his side.

"And since my family is in the UAE, I'll be going with him," Tahira said.

"I'm hopping a train in less than an hour," Adam said, tugging a pair of cotton gloves onto his hands. "That's why I had to bring this." He gestured toward the Atherton-Pryce duffel bouncing against his hip. Sticking out of the outside pocket was a copy of a local newspaper, and a smaller headline caught Ariana's eye.

GEORGETOWN SOCCER STAR INJURED IN CRASH

"Adam, do you mind if I . . . ?"

Hands trembling, Ariana plucked the paper from the pocket.

"Sure," Adam said. "Go ahead."

Ariana stepped carefully, keeping pace with her friends as she scanned the article. Her eyes instantly found Reed's name and her mouth went dry. Apparently, one of her teammates had gotten drunk and tried to drive home from a party. That was why Reed had been at the hospital the other night.

What are the chances? Ariana thought now, carefully folding the paper and handing it back to Adam. *What are the chances that we would both end up in the same ER on the same night because our friends were hurt?*

It was fate. It had to be. Someone had put Reed right in front of her that night for a reason. All of this was Reed's fault, after all. If Reed had never come to Easton Academy in the first place, Thomas Pearson would still be alive. If Thomas were alive, Ariana never would have gone to the Brenda T. and met Kaitlynn Nottingham. If she'd never met Kaitlynn, she never would have known Briana Leigh Covington existed. Briana Leigh's death was on Reed's head. As was Brigit Rhygstead's, and Lexa's as well. Clearly, Reed had been placed in that ER on that very night because the universe was trying to balance itself. The universe wanted Reed dead.

She must die . . . she must die . . . she must die . . .

"Come on. We'll drop you off at the station on our way back to campus," Jasper offered to Adam.

"Cool, thanks," Adam said, smiling gratefully.

Ariana forced herself to look straight ahead and not stare at the newspaper now coiled into a tube in Adam's hands. The universe was trying to tell her something, and she had now gotten the message loud and clear.

It all came back to Reed Brennan.

Kill Reed and all these deaths would be avenged. Kill Reed, and there would finally, *finally* be justice.

As she popped open the door of her silver Porsche, Ariana felt much calmer and completely resolved. She would go back to her dorm, finish packing for Jasper's, and spend the rest of the afternoon until her flight working on the Reed problem. The worst was over. It was time to focus. Ariana Osgood had a job to do.

UNCLE JAZZ

"Uncle Jazz! Uncle Jazz! Look what I made for you!"

Jasper's adorable, towheaded nephew, Ben, came tearing into the banquet-size dining room in the Montgomerys' stately southern mansion, proudly carrying a mishmash of Play-Doh. Around the table, the adults still lingered over coffee and pie. Ariana sat next to Jasper on one side of the festively decorated table, with his older sister Jacqueline to her left. Across the way, Ben's parents sat, watching their progeny proudly. Jasper's oldest sister, Jessica, was massively pregnant once again, and her husband, Sherman, hadn't let go of her hand for more than thirty seconds all night. At the head and foot of the table were Jasper's parents: Mr. Montgomery pushed back from his plate to make more room for his ample belly; Mrs. Montgomery perched at the edge of her chair as she sipped her coffee. Ben had long since vacated the dining room, unable to sit still, and had been occupying himself with his Play-Doh in the parlor for the last half hour.

"Wow!" Jasper crowed, pulling Ben into his lap. "That is the scariest looking monster I've ever seen!"

Ariana smiled. Jasper was so cute with Ben, it made her heart hurt.

Ben's face, however, fell like a stone. "It's not a monster," he said, fiddling with one of the buttons on Jasper's Ralph Lauren shirt. "It's you!"

Jasper hesitated a second as Jessica covered up a laugh, but he recovered quickly.

"And as we all know, I'm the scariest monster south of the Mason-Dixon line!" he said, opening his eyes wide and letting out a growl.

Ben half screamed, half giggled, and wriggled off Jasper's lap, sprinting back for the parlor. Jasper gave chase, leaving Ariana alone at the table with his family. She sighed contentedly and added some sugar to her coffee. Outside the huge bay window, a grassy hill descended toward a lily pad–spotted pond, its water gleaming in the waning November sunlight. There were several Adirondack chairs set up around a huge stone fire pit, where Jasper had promised the family would repose later that night to roast marshmallows and tell stories. Ariana couldn't have imagined a more perfect way to end a perfect day.

"Well, Jessie, if the one in your belly's half as much of a hoot as *that* one, things are about to get a heck of a lot livelier around here," Mr. Montgomery said, lifting his bushy eyebrows.

Jessica blew out her cheeks and ran her hand over her bump. "Well, she doesn't stop kicking me, so I think we're in for it."

Everyone laughed lightly. Ariana felt Mrs. Montgomery's eyes on her cheek and looked down at her untouched pecan pie.

"You've been rather quiet since dinner was cleared, Ana," Jasper's mother said. "Is everything all right?"

"Oh, yes. Of course. Thanks," Ariana said, coloring slightly. She felt the warm glow of the taper candles on her face. "It's just . . . it's been a long time since I've had a real family Thanksgiving."

Ariana watched as the members of Jasper's family exchanged wary looks. She knew instantly that they had discussed Briana Leigh's history and that, quite possibly, Jasper had warned them against saying anything that might make her uncomfortable or sad.

Just like Jasper.

"What did you and your folks used to do for Thanksgiving?" Jessica asked.

Her mother shot her a warning look, but Ariana suddenly realized she wouldn't mind reminiscing about her parents a bit. Usually she refused to let herself even think about them, but something about today had put her in a nostalgic mood, and she felt safe among Jasper's family.

"I didn't have a huge extended family, but my mother always invited over all the neighbors," Ariana said. "Anyone who didn't have a place to go was welcome at our house."

"That sounds nice," Jacqueline said. "Like what Thanksgiving's really supposed to be about."

"It *was* nice," Ariana said with a soft smile. "The only thing I didn't like was that my mother didn't cook that night. She always hired in. I understand why—she wanted to be able to spend time with us instead of in the kitchen—but she was an amazing cook. She used to make this rosemary garlic chicken with mashed potatoes and southern biscuits from scratch. That was always my favorite meal growing up."

"Now you're making me hungry again," Sherman joked, patting his flat stomach with his free hand.

Everyone laughed and Ariana blushed. "Sorry. I'm rambling."

"Not at all, Ana," Mrs. Montgomery said with a kind smile, her coiffed blond hair so full of product, it sat motionless as she nodded at Ariana. "And I want you to know that as much as I'm sure you miss your family, we're all very happy to have you here."

"Jazz calls me to brag about you, like, every day at school," Jacqueline informed her with a smile. "He's annoying the heck out of my roommate."

Ariana's chest inflated with happiness. Until recently, she had no idea Jasper's sisters even knew she existed. It meant a lot that he spoke to them about her so often.

Mr. Montgomery cleared his throat and leaned forward, resting his elbows on the pristine white tablecloth.

"I remember reading about your father's death at the time," he said, pressing his hands together. "Awful business. Awful business."

"Yes," Ariana said, casting her eyes down again.

"I hope they put away the psycho that did it," he said.

"Thurston!" Mrs. Montgomery scolded.

"What? I'm just offering my support!" he said, turning his massive palms up.

"It's okay," Ariana said, slowly stirring her coffee and trying as hard as she could not to grin. "Let's just say she was properly punished."

She thought of Kaitlynn Nottingham rotting in the cold hard ground behind the Greene's Washington mansion and fancied the real Briana Leigh and her father would agree.

"Good. I'm always gratified to hear that justice was served," Mr. Montgomery said.

Now Ariana smiled hugely. She knew she liked Jasper's father. Suddenly she felt even more comfortable with the idea of sharing the long weekend with him and his family.

"Thank you for your restraint, people," Jasper said lightly from the doorway, crossing his arms over his chest. "You lasted a whole twenty-four hours before broaching the exact unpleasantness I asked you not to broach."

Jasper's father started to turn in his seat to retort, but Ariana cut him off.

"It's all right, Jasper," Ariana said. "I don't mind at all."

With a discreet eye roll, Jasper sat down next to Ariana again, placing his napkin back in his lap and taking Ariana's hand in his under the table. Ariana squeezed his fingers, a wave of contentment warming every inch of her skin. She loved him so much for trying to protect her, even though he knew he didn't really have to. He knew she could take care of herself, but he still wanted to take care of her. Looking around at his family, at the playfully scolding look his mom was shooting at his dad, at the way Sherman and Jessica constantly whispered with each other, she could see how he'd grown up so attentive and caring.

For the first time in forever, Ariana felt like part of a family. It was a feeling she wanted more than anything to hold on to, and she had Jasper to thank for it.

A PLAN

The cold emanating from the stone bench had long since permeated Ariana's bones. The latte she'd purchased from the coffee cart mere minutes ago—her fifth of the day—had already gone lukewarm in her hands. The skin around her mouth and eyes was so dry she could feel it cracking as she attempted to imagine herself on a warm beach somewhere. Attempted to put mind over matter.

This was no way to spend a Sunday evening.

"Where the hell is she?" Ariana said under her breath.

A pair of sorority types walking by, dragging small rolling luggage cases, shot her a disturbed glance. She supposed she looked rather odd, sitting there in a brand-new Georgetown baseball cap and huge Gucci sunglasses after dark, talking to no one. Ariana took a long sip of her coffee, covering as much of her face as she could, and pretended not to notice. She was not supposed to be bringing attention to herself. But, she supposed, lapses in judgment were to be expected after five hours of sitting still on one's ass on a frigid, sunless November day.

Ariana and Jasper had arrived back on campus that morning after three straight days of eating, laughing, and partying with his family. It had been a whirlwind of good food, good music, and bonding with Jasper's mother and sisters, and by the time they had reached Privilege House, all she'd felt like doing was curling into a ball for some sleep. But she had more important things to do. Tonight would be the perfect night to pinpoint where on campus Reed lived, as she was sure to be returning from some awful white-trash Thanksgiving in Backwater, PA.

Now, all these hours later, Ariana was fairly certain she'd seen every single undergrad return from their holiday except Reed. Where the hell was she? Was Turkey Day in the middle of nowhere really so much fun that she wanted to drag it out as long as possible?

Ariana took a calming breath and blew it out. She had narrowed Reed's potential places of residence to three dorms within a half-mile radius of one another. Unfortunately, the front doors of these establishments all faced in various directions, so Ariana hadn't been able to choose one vantage point. She had begun her day outside the first dorm and had watched dozens of freshman girls come and go, but Reed was not among them. Around five p.m., Ariana had decided to move on to dorm number two. At one point Ariana had spotted a klatch of girls in soccer jackets, but Reed wasn't there. Finally, at seven, freezing and frustrated, Ariana had taken up her current position outside the third and final dorm. At this point she was hungry, jittery from all the caffeine, and feeling so thwarted that she was ready to throttle the first tall brunette that crossed her path.

What if she had missed her? What if the girl was, right now, returning to that first dorm, out of sight? If Ariana had to come back in the morning and start this process all over again, she might have a nervous breakdown.

Suddenly, her phone beeped, startling her. Ariana placed her coffee cup down next to her and pulled the cell from her pocket, being careful to keep one eye on the door of the dorm. The text was from Jasper.

COME BACK SOON. IT'S COLD HERE WITHOUT YOU.

Ariana smiled. He'd been sending her romantic little texts all afternoon, but never asked her where she was or what she was doing. It was so nice to have a boyfriend who wasn't nosy or demanding or controlling. All he wanted was to be with her.

BACK SOON. PROMISE.

Ariana hit SEND and slipped the phone back into her pocket. She was just about done here anyway. Clearly mere surveillance wasn't going to be enough. She was going to have to figure out some other, more efficient way to determine where Reed was staying. Maybe she could devise a way to hack into the school's system. Or simply fly to that awful town where Reed hailed from and ask her parents. They were probably just hick-dumb enough to tell her.

With a sigh, Ariana pushed herself to her feet, her frozen muscles and bones cracking and protesting. She was just about to head for the visitor's lot when she heard a laugh that stopped her cold.

Slowly, Ariana looked up, and there she was. Reed Brennan in the flesh. She was walking with three friends about twenty yards away, tugging along a rolling suitcase, headed toward the dorm. And just in case Ariana was concerned that her mind was messing with her again, Reed was wearing a vinyl warm-up jacket with her last name emblazoned across the back in huge letters.

Suddenly, Ariana's mouth filled with saliva. She swallowed hard, disgusted. It was amazing, the effect Reed had on her. It was all Ariana could do to stop herself from sprinting across the quad and launching herself at the girl like a wild animal. The primal beat started up inside of her all over again, this time louder than ever.

She must die . . . she must die . . . she must die . . .

At the front door of the dorm, Reed paused and tugged a key card out of her pocket.

She must die . . . she must die . . . she must die . . .

Reed flashed the card in front of the electronic pad, then reached over and opened the door for her friends.

She must die . . . she must die . . . she must die . . .

They all piled inside, Reed at the rear, and the door slammed behind them.

Ariana blinked, waking up from her trance. Reed was gone, and that was that. Ariana breathed in, long and slow, and felt her pulse start to slow. Reed had a key to the building, so this was clearly where she lived. Now all Ariana had to do was watch her, get her schedule down, and figure out the optimal moment to attack.

Soon, it would all be over. Soon, the balance would be restored. All the deaths—Thomas's, Briana Leigh's, Brigit's, Lexa's—all of them would be avenged.

Lifting her chin, Ariana turned and calmly strode toward the parking lot. Her heart rate was perfectly calm. Her breathing perfectly normal. This time she was going to have a plan. A foolproof plan. This time she was going to leave nothing to chance like when she'd done away with that horrible Mel girl back in Easton, or poor Sergei at the lake, or the first time she'd tried to kill Kaitlynn in her hotel room on Dupont Circle, or that awful, fateful night when she'd come so close to pushing Reed off the roof of Billings House.

It was always much better to have a plan. And this was far too important to leave anything to chance.

THE NOMINATION

"I now open the floor to official nominations for the post of President of the Atherton-Pryce Hall chapter of Stone and Grave."

April's words brought a chill over the membership, and for a long moment, no one said a word. It was as if no one wanted to be the first to suggest that someone could actually replace Lexa. Ariana's eyes scanned the circle, which was again devoid of Palmer and Conrad, and this time Soomie as well. No one had been able to get in touch with Soomie over the Thanksgiving break, but Maria had been hopeful that she would return to campus today just like everyone else. Unfortunately, she'd never arrived, and when Ariana and Maria had gone to her room before leaving for this meeting, just to be sure, everything was dark. Stone and Grave's numbers were slowly dwindling and it felt as if nothing would ever be the same.

Finally, Landon cleared his throat. It was such a surprise, and so close to Ariana's ear, that she flinched away.

"I nominate Brother Starbuck," Landon said, gazing defiantly at

Maria from across the circle. Ariana sighed. Apparently they were picking up right where they'd left off.

"I second it," Christian Thacker called out.

"Fine." April made a note in a black cloth book she had open across her lap. "Any other nominations?"

"I nominate Sister Miss Temple," Maria said, smiling at April.

Kassie went to second it, but April shook her head.

"Sorry, but I decline the nomination," she said. "I have way too much on my plate right now to take that on too."

Tahira raised her hand.

"Sister Sister Carrie?" April called on her.

At Ariana's other side, Landon snorted. Ariana smirked. The repetition in Tahira's Stone and Grave name *was* kind of funny. She was glad she hadn't been saddled with it.

"I nominate Sister Portia," Tahira said, leaning back to grin at Ariana.

"What?" Ariana breathed, shocked.

Ariana glanced at Jasper as a round of whispers moved swiftly through the room, echoing off the domed ceiling. He grinned back at her and raised his hand.

"Seconded!" he said loudly.

"But she's a new member," April said, her pen poised over the book. Ariana's face turned to stone.

"Sorry. I was just surprised," April said quickly, noticing Ariana's reaction. "It's just . . . that's never been done before."

"Well there's a first time for everything," Adam piped up. "And

Ana . . . I mean, Sister Portia, was the MVP of our pledge class." He raised his hand, leaning forward in the circle so he could see Ariana. "I second the nomination, too. Or third it. Whatever."

There was a grumble among some of the seniors, but no one objected.

"All right then," April said with a smile. "Sister Portia has been nominated."

Ariana held her breath as the tip of the pen scratched across the paper. She beamed at Tahira, her face, she was sure, burning bright red. She couldn't believe she'd just been nominated for president of Stone and Grave. It was not only the highest position in the secret society, but considering how exclusive S and G was, it was basically the highest position in all the school. And Tahira, Adam, and Jasper thought she deserved to have it.

"Any other nominations?" April asked.

Landon sighed. Christian cracked his knuckles. Otherwise, the cave was silent as a tomb.

"All right then. We'll hold a special election at our next meeting," April said, slapping the book closed. "Thank you all for coming at such short notice. Meeting adjourned."

As everyone scrambled to their feet, Jasper, Tahira, Maria, Rob, and a few other members gathered around Ariana to congratulate her. Ariana tried to look solemn, tried to appear as if this was all a lot to take in—the idea of replacing her best friend. But inside, she had never been so excited. As she looked into Jasper's proud, admiring eyes and squeezed his hand, she felt as if all her dreams were coming true.

BENEVOLENT

Ariana walked across campus toward the dining hall before lunch on Monday afternoon, feeling as if people were already starting to look at her differently. All morning, girls from Stone and Grave had been coming up to her, swearing their allegiance, promising to vote for her at Wednesday's midnight gathering. With each new promise, Ariana felt her chest inflate a bit more. She looked around at the red brick buildings of campus, the piles of colorful leaves gathered alongside the slate walks, the blue-and-gray APH flag whipping from every hall's flagpole, and felt as if the crisp fall air was filling her from the inside, bringing all sorts of possibilities.

I'm going to own *this place,* Ariana thought, pausing near the steps of the administration building. *All I need are a few more votes and this school, these students, the world . . . may as well be mine.*

She licked her lips, wondering what sorts of perks the president of Stone and Grave could expect to enjoy. Lexa had never talked much about it, or at all. She had taken her position of power and prestige in stride, as if it was simply part of who she was, not something to be wielded or shown off. Thinking of Lexa's mature demeanor now, Ariana vowed to herself that she would be the same way. She would not abuse her power, nor would she cause anyone to feel envious or covetous of her position. She would be a good, kind, benevolent leader.

If, of course, she won.

Ariana smiled at Quinn, who waved as she went by. She pulled her cell phone out of her bag to see if Soomie had responded to any of the many texts she had sent that morning between classes. There were some new texts, but they were all from Jasper, Maria, and Tahira.

Biting her lip, Ariana speed-dialed Soomie's cell. The voice mail had already picked up by the time she'd brought her phone to her ear.

"You know what to do at the beep!" Soomie said brightly.

"Soomie, it's Ana," Ariana said, turning and moseying up the walk with a leisurely gait, enjoying the feeling of the sun on her face. "I'm sure you're tired of Maria and me stalking you, but we're both really worried. Just . . . give one of us a call back as soon as you can. We don't need to have some long, drawn-out talk or anything. We just want to know you're okay."

And also, it would be nice if you could come back to campus and vote for me Wednesday night, she added silently.

She racked her brain for a way to say this without really saying it, but came up blank.

"Okay, well. Hope to see you soon!"

She hung up the phone feeling frustrated and concerned. Of course Soomie was upset. First her best friend Brigit had fallen to her death, and now Lexa. Not everyone could take such awful tragedies in stride. Ariana just hoped that wherever she was, she wasn't going to do anything stupid.

The last thing she needed was another death to avenge.

Suddenly, a dog's bark split the cold air. Ariana's pulse completely stopped, then thumped back up to a frightening pace. She whirled around, searching the campus for the source of the noise.

The bark sounded familiar. Too familiar. Every inch of Ariana's skin tingled. The tiny hairs on the back of her neck stood on end. Where was it coming from? The sound seemed to echo off every wall, coming at her from all angles. She had to see the dog. She had to make sure it wasn't—

And then, suddenly, the barking stopped.

Ariana narrowed her eyes, scanning the campus, but there were no canines in sight. The fist of fear that gripped Ariana's heart loosened slightly. She was just hearing things, clearly. All these thoughts of Reed and Briana Leigh and avenging deaths were starting to fool with her mind. That's all it was.

Ariana lifted her chin as she turned her steps back toward the dining hall.

All she had to do was get rid of Reed and all this insanity would stop. Get rid of Reed, and everything would be all right.

THE WRONG GIRL

She must die . . . she must die . . . she must die . . .

Ariana followed twenty paces behind Reed on Tuesday as she made her way back from her second class of the day and toward her dorm. After calling in sick—so early she'd gotten the nurse's voice mail—she'd snuck out of Privilege House, to her car, and through the gates. She'd arrived at Georgetown within half an hour, at exactly 5:30 a.m., just in time to see Reed walk out the front door of her dorm and take off on an hour-long jog. After that, she'd returned to her dorm and emerged two hours later, traipsing along the path in a camel coat with two of her healthy, fresh-faced friends at her sides. Now it was one o'clock, and Reed hadn't once glanced over her shoulder, hadn't looked around suspiciously, hadn't suspected she was being watched. The girl had no instincts. No intuition. A major defect, as far as Ariana was concerned.

Reed used her key card and stepped inside the dorm. Ariana leaned back against the trunk of a nearby oak tree and whipped out the small notebook she'd purchased at the campus bookstore that morning while Reed was in class. In it were her meticulous notes.

5:30–6:32: Jogs around campus. Returns to dorm via dark alleyway (POSS)

8:30–8:34: Walks to dining hall

8:34–9:15: Breakfast with friends

9:15–9:20: Walks to English class, takes public route through quad (NG)

9:25–10:30: Endures most boring lecture on Shakespeare ever

10:30–10:37: Walks to gym, cuts through deserted parking lot (POSS)

10:45–11:30: Lifts weights (EW)

11:30–11:45: Showers and changes, not many people in gym at this hour (SHOWERS, POSS?)

11:45–11:55: Walks to biology class, another public route (NG)

12:00–12:43: Takes biology exam. Fifth student to finish

12:43–12:52: Walks to dorm, cuts behind the biology building, passing only one other student (POSS?)

Satisfied that her notes were concise and clear, Ariana tucked the notebook away and checked her phone. There was a text from Tahira.

STOPPED BY W/BAGEL. WHERE R U? PLAYING HOOKY? WANT CMPNY?

Ariana thought about texting back, but decided against it. She was planning on spending her entire day here at Georgetown. She had a lot of work to do.

Tahira texted again.

WHERE R U?????

Ariana groaned and tucked her phone away. Maybe she'd tell

Tahira she'd sat in movie theaters all day and turned off her phone.

The front door of the dorm popped open and Reed walked out, chatting on her cell. Instead of turning to the right, as she had done every other time that day, Reed walked up the path directly in front of her. The path that would lead her straight past Ariana's tree. Heart in her throat, Ariana turned to the side and leaned her shoulder against the rough bark of the tree trunk. She whipped out a worn copy of *Catch-22* and held it up to her face, pretending to be engrossed.

"Are you kidding?" Reed said into the phone with a laugh. "My parents are *psyched* to spend New Year's at the Cape. My mom doesn't have to worry about making plans and my dad is all about skeet shooting with your father. He bought a vest and everything."

Ariana bit down hard on her tongue. Bit down until she tasted blood. Reed was passing by just a few feet away. Mere inches. What she wouldn't give to just reach out and grab her. Cover her mouth and pinch her nose closed. Drag her behind the tree and hold her down and press and press and press until she stopped struggling.

"Josh! Shut up! No, we are not sharing a room," Reed screeched, laughing like a hyena.

A chill raced down the back of Ariana's neck. Reed was talking to Josh Hollis? It made sense, she supposed. His parents did have a gorgeous, sprawling house at Cape Cod. But really. Those two were still together? How was that even possible? Josh was a good guy. Smart and kind and big-hearted. How had Reed managed not to irritate him to within an inch of his sanity by now?

"I know, I know," Reed said. "I love you, too."

She hung up the phone and kept walking toward the dining hall. As Ariana slipped away from her tree, she felt an odd pang of sympathy deep within her chest. Poor Josh. He'd be so sad when he found out Reed was dead.

But then, it was his own fault. There was always a price to pay for getting involved with the wrong girl.

BLAST FROM THE PAST

As Ariana walked out of the Privilege House café, she popped the top off her vanilla latte and took a nice, long whiff of the sweet, comforting scent. Slowly, her shoulder muscles started to uncoil. It had been a long, cold day. She'd had a lot of success, of course—nailing down Reed's schedule, getting some ideas as to where, when, and how the deed could be done—but by the time it was over, she felt frozen from the inside out. Now that she was back home, she deserved a little downtime.

Halfway across the common room to the lobby, Ariana caught a glimpse of April's red curls inside the lounge. She was sitting on one of the couches with the TV tuned to the news, which seemed to be covering one of the charitable stories of the season—all fresh-faced kids and lovingly wrapped presents. Ariana smiled, seeing a perfect opportunity to nail down April's currently iffy Stone and Grave vote. Apparently the downtime would have to be put off a bit.

But the moment she was through the door of the lounge, she stopped in her tracks. Seated on the couch in front of the second flat-screen TV were Palmer, Christian, Rob, and Landon, playing a raucous game of *Call of Duty*. The last thing she wanted was to be around Palmer, and she almost backed out again, but then he turned and saw her. His face was covered in day-old stubble and he wore a rumpled V-neck sweater, but was still annoyingly hot. He gave her a cursory, dismissive glance and returned his attention to the game. Ariana's face burned. As much as she wanted to, she couldn't leave now. She couldn't let him have the satisfaction.

"Hi, April," she said brightly, walking around the side of the couch. She plopped down next to the senior, disturbing the binder she had open across her lap and ruffling some papers. "Oh, I'm sorry. I didn't realize you were studying."

"I'm not," April replied, heaving a sigh. "I'm trying to organize all these submissions for the lit magazine." She lifted a sheaf of papers in one hand. "Hasn't anyone at this school ever heard of e-mail?"

Ariana smirked and took a sip of her latte. "Need help?"

"Yes, please, thank you," April said in one breath. She handed a disorganized stack of submissions to Ariana. "I'm starting by sorting them into piles by format. This one's poetry and that one's fiction," she said, pointing to two separate stacks placed on the couch at her sides.

Ariana put her coffee down on the glass coffee table, and noticed another pile of looseleaf and printer paper there. "What's that?" she asked, as the guys on the other couch shouted over a huge explosion.

April rolled her eyes behind her tortoiseshell glasses. "Unknown format."

Ariana laughed. "I don't even want to know."

"And now, a breaking news story from our nation's capital," the newscaster on the television announced. Ariana and April both looked up, and Palmer glanced over from the opposite couch. "This afternoon, a grizzly discovery was made on the banks of the Potomac River as the body of a young woman washed up on shore."

The back of Ariana's skull went fuzzy and weightless. It wasn't. It couldn't be.

"Pause the game," Palmer ordered.

Rob did as he was told and Palmer got up, then lowered himself onto the arm of the couch, facing April's TV. On the screen, a half dozen police loaded a black body bag into the back of the ambulance on the banks of a river.

"The remains have been identified as those of international fashion model, Kiran Hayes," the newscaster's voiceover continued. Ariana's blood turned to icy slush as suddenly Kiran Hayes's smiling face grinned out at her.

"Oh my God," she uttered, her hand flying to her mouth.

"What?" April said. "Ana? Are you all right?"

"M'fine," Ariana mumbled, even as her life flashed before her eyes. How had they found her body? How? It had been weeks since she'd shoved a very drunk Kiran off a bridge into the raging Potomac on Halloween night. Ariana had thought that with each passing day she was safer and safer from her former friend's body ever being found.

And now, there Kiran was in the flesh and larger than life, strutting down a Fashion Week runway, posing with other models for a makeup ad, getting out of a limo with some half-wasted Hollywood B-lister.

"Widely acknowledged to be one of high fashion's rising stars, Miss Hayes has not been seen or heard from since Halloween night, when she called an old friend from her former prep school, Easton Academy."

Now the guys were fully interested, murmuring and conjecturing as they realized that Kiran was one of their own ilk.

"Shhh!" Ariana said, holding out a hand.

She caught a few confused looks, but everyone quieted down. On the screen flashed a photograph of Kiran and Noelle taken in front of Billings during Kiran's junior year. The photo had been cropped, but a hand hung around Kiran's shoulder in the center of the picture. Ariana nearly blacked out at the sight of it. It was her own slim, pale hand. If they'd shown the entire shot . . .

If they'd shown the entire shot, everyone in the room would have seen it. Every single one of them would have recognized her.

"And while this looks like a possible accident, police have yet to rule out foul play," the newscaster was saying. "For WDCW news, I'm Melinda Chang."

Ariana stood up shakily, strewing papers all over the floor at her feet. She turned away from the screen and stumbled back toward the lobby. Foul play. They hadn't ruled out foul play. Had she left some kind of evidence on Kiran? A fingerprint? A fiber? A hair?

"Where're you going?" Palmer demanded.

Ariana froze. Her spine felt like a long strip of ice. "What?" she said, turning to him.

"That's the most emotion I've seen from you since your so-called best friend died," he said belligerently, approaching her. "How is it you're crying over some dead model when I've never seen you shed a tear over Lexa?"

"Leave me alone," Ariana said through her teeth. She could not deal with Palmer and his bruised feelings right now. She started to go again, but he grabbed her arm.

"No. I don't think so," Palmer said. "You were the last one to see her alive, you know. What did she say to you? What did you do? Did you upset her or something? What happened in that room?"

"Palmer," April said, her voice aghast. "You can't really think—"

"I don't have to tell you anything," Ariana replied, clenching her teeth as hard as she could to keep from exploding, to keep herself under control. "But just FYI, even if we did have an upsetting conversation, that can't cause an aneurysm."

"How can you joke about this?" Palmer spat. "You don't care about anyone but yourself. Not even your dead best friend."

"Dude," Landon said.

Ariana glanced at him over Palmer's shoulder. Even Palmer flinched. If Landon thought he was out of line, he must have done something really wrong. Before another word could be uttered, Ariana turned on her heel, forcing her chin up, and walked away. But by the time she got to the elevators, she was shaking from head to toe.

Palmer had come far too close to the truth for her comfort. Did he truly suspect something? And what about this foul play allegation that Chang woman mentioned on the news? Did the police really suspect that Kiran had been murdered? If so, how long did she have before they came banging down her door?

As the doors slid open, Ariana stepped inside and tried to breathe.

Kiran's body had spent five weeks at the bottom of a river. There couldn't possibly be anything left that could lead them to Briana Leigh Covington or Ariana Osgood.

Could there?

CATHARSIS

Ariana let out a cathartic screech as she smacked the small blue ball with the overly used, seriously abused racquetball racket. The ball slammed against the white wall and thwacked against the gleaming wood floor, ricocheting toward the far side of the two-story-high enclosed court. Ariana sprinted to reach it, her sneakers screeching along the boards, her breath coming quick and heavy. She reached back and executed a perfect return, sending the ball back to the wall. Overhead, one of the fluorescent lights flickered, but she ignored it and returned the ball again. Right now, she was focused, and nothing could distract her.

Then, the door to the racquetball court squeaked open, and her ball went flying out into the lobby.

"Whoa!" Maria blurted, jumping out of the projectile's path. "Sorry."

"S'okay," Ariana said, trying to catch her breath.

She walked over to her bag, wiped her sweaty face with a towel, and grabbed the tube of balls she'd purchased at the gym store before starting her game. They hadn't had any women's rackets left for sale—thus the borrowed, used racket—but at least she'd been able to pop open a fresh sleeve of balls.

"Mind if I join you?" Maria asked, wielding her own borrowed racket. She was wearing short cotton shorts and a gray tank top and already had a patch of sweat on her stomach and another across her chest. Her hair was back in a messy ponytail, and she clasped an iPod in her other hand. Clearly she'd already been working out for a while when she'd noticed Ariana on the racquetball court.

"Not at all," Ariana said, still catching her breath.

Maria put her iPod down atop Ariana's bag and jogged in place a bit, her ponytail dancing from shoulder to shoulder.

"I don't think I've ever seen you inside the gym before," she commented, eyeing Ariana's tennis whites—a straight white skirt with one pleat and a long-sleeved white polo shirt over Nike tennis sneakers.

"That's because I've never been here before," Ariana said as she bounced the ball atop her racket. "But tonight, I just felt a dire need to hit something, and the lights weren't on at the tennis courts, so here I am."

"Yeah, I guess when it's thirty degrees outside they figure no one's going to be up for tennis after dark," Maria joked, joining Ariana at the service line.

"They thought wrong," she replied, without a trace of mirth. Ever since she'd seen Kiran's face on the news earlier that evening, not a positive, light, or happy thought had passed through her mind. It was all panic, conjecture, worry, and fear. Which was why she was here, sweating it out, trying to clear her mind. "Play to fifteen?" she asked Maria.

"Sure," Maria said, bending at the waist and shifting her weight from one leg to the other.

Ariana smirked. Maria was a skinny, frail ballerina. There was no way she played racquetball on a regular basis. This was going to be one easy win.

She tossed the ball up and served. Maria returned it with a formidable swing. The ball hit the wall, then the floor and whizzed right toward Ariana, but about three feet above her head. She jumped up and lobbed a return, but it felt short.

"My serve," Maria said, retrieving the ball.

"Nice shot," Ariana said, impressed but also slightly annoyed.

Maria tilted her head modestly. "Thanks."

She bounced the ball a few times at her feet. "I'm worried about Soomie. I don't think we've ever gone this long without talking or e-mailing or texting or *something*."

With a quick toss, she served the ball. Ariana returned it cleanly, so fast Maria had no time to react, and it ricocheted off her thigh.

"Ow! That's gonna leave a mark," Maria said, rubbing the spot with the flat of her hand.

"Sorry," Ariana said, jogging to pick up the ball.

"Hazards of the sport, I guess," Maria said lightly. "So you still haven't heard from her?"

"No. I'm worried too. It's not like her to just disappear and not even leave a note. She's too . . ."

"OCD?" Maria joked.

Ariana laughed, surprising herself. "That's the acronym I was looking for."

Maria smiled and Ariana served. They were quiet for a few minutes as they ran around the court after the ball, ducking one another, racing for the walls. Eventually, Ariana caught a perfect angle and won the point.

"Whoo! Nice one!" Maria said, raising her hand for a high five.

Ariana had never high-fived anyone in her life. Now she shrugged one shoulder and slapped Maria's hand. They both laughed. They looked into one another's eyes and suddenly, Ariana couldn't stop smiling.

"I see what you mean about needing to hit something," Maria said, getting poised for another return. "I already feel loads better."

Ariana took a quick swig of water from her water bottle, then returned to the service line. "Then we should do this more often."

Maria grinned. "Works for me."

Ariana grinned back and, feeling suddenly like she had been crazy to ever worry that anything could really go wrong, she tossed the ball up to serve.

THE DUNGEON

Ariana sat at a table in the Georgetown dining hall on Wednesday morning, her nose buried in her Atherton-Pryce chemistry book, which was definitely hefty enough to pass as a college text. To any casual passerby, she looked like a student who had pulled an all-nighter and was now nursing a coffee and getting in some last-minute cramming. In fact, every ounce of her attention was tuned to the conversation taking place at the table behind her.

"I can't believe she's really dead," Reed said, sniffling. "We figured she'd just met some hot guy and disappeared to Tahiti for a few weeks."

Ariana smiled sadly. That *did* sound like Kiran.

"I'm so sorry, Reed," one of her friends said.

Ariana had seen Reed walk in, all red-nosed, wearing a baggy Georgetown sweatshirt and no makeup, surrounded by concerned tomboys. She imagined one of them putting an arm around her now, giving her a supportive squeeze. As if Kiran and Reed had ever really been friends. Ariana had known Kiran much longer, and if Reed could have heard some of the crap Kiran had talked about her and her wardrobe behind her back, she wouldn't be so mournful right now.

"I wonder how it happened," another friend chimed in.

Ariana's ears perked up as Reed scoffed derisively.

"My friend Noelle heard she was really wasted at the Halloween party she was at," she said. "Classic Kiran. Apparently the police think she must have been so drunk she tripped and fell in the water," she added, her tone bitter.

Ariana let out a sigh of relief unlike any other. If this was true, she was in the clear. *Thank you, Kiran, for your hedonistic ways.* But then a sour taste filled her mouth, tempering her happiness as Reed's comment about Noelle really hit her. So. Reed and Noelle were still friends.

"Crap. I have to get to class," one of Reed's entourage said. A chair scraped back. "Hey . . . you guys are going to that team breakfast thing on Friday, right?"

There was a chorus of assenting murmurs.

"I can't," Reed said. "I'm so behind in bio and I've got that lab due on Friday morning. I'm going to be spending every free second in the lab until first session starts."

"You're going to the dungeon, alone, *before* class on a Friday?" one of the friends asked incredulously. "Are you crazy?"

"I know. That place freaks me out even in the middle of the day," Reed replied. "But I have to ace this lab. It's, like, fifty percent of my final grade."

A sizzle of anticipation shot up and down Ariana's arms. This dungeon lab place sounded like a perfect location for her purposes. And from the tone of the friend's voice, it would be completely deserted early on a Friday morning, which made perfect sense. Thursday night was the requisite party night on college campuses. Only a loser with no life would drag themselves out of bed before dawn on a Friday and into a lab. A loser like Reed. Ariana would have to check out this so-called dungeon after Reed went to class today. But if it was as cold and dark and quiet and windowless as she was currently imagining . . . she'd just caught the break she'd been hoping for.

A LOCK

"Are you nervous?" Jasper asked Ariana, sliding into the chair next to hers in the dining hall that night.

The very word "nervous" sent a whole new shockwave of prickling discomfort over Ariana's shoulders and down her arms. In just a few hours the Stone and Grave vote would finally take place. She'd thought of little else all day, but he didn't need to know that. Ariana took a deep breath and shrugged casually.

"Not at all," she said, reaching for a warm roll from the basket at the center of the table. The waiter had yet to come and take her order, but it was no matter. She was certain she wouldn't be able to eat much anyway.

"Liar." Jasper planted a kiss on her cheek as he stashed his leather messenger bag under the table. "Personally, I think you're a lock."

Ariana's eyebrows shot up. "You do? What have you heard?"

"Nothing really. But why would anyone *not* vote for you?" Jasper replied, flicking his napkin into his lap.

Ariana shook her head with a smile. "You're my boyfriend. You have to say that," she whispered, eyeing Palmer and Landon as they strode by. Landon lifted his hand briefly in greeting, but Palmer didn't even cast a glance in their direction.

"Cocky bastard. He deserves to be brought down a peg," Jasper muttered.

Ariana clenched her teeth, recalling the look in Palmer's eyes as he'd accused her the night before. "I couldn't agree more."

April dropped into the chair across from Jasper's, struggling to detangle the straps of the tote bag, duffel, and backpack she was carrying. She finally got it all organized, shoved the bags under her chair, and took a deep breath.

"Ready for tonight?" she asked Ariana.

"Ready as I'm gonna be," Ariana replied.

April touched the silverware lined up next to her plate, straightening them into right angles. "I have to admit, Ana, up until last night I was still on the fence about the vote," she said, sitting up straight and shaking her curls back from her face. "I mean, you are new and all. But there's no way I can vote for a jerk like him," she said, casting a derisive look in Palmer's direction as he settled in at a table near the end of the row. "And the way you handled it? Perfection."

"Thanks," Ariana said, blushing as she looked down at her lap.

"Wait a minute. What happened last night?" Jasper asked, angling toward Ariana in his chair. "What did the jerk do?"

"Nothing," Ariana said quickly, shaking her head.

"Oh, bollocks. It was *not* nothing," April said. She placed her elbows on the table and leaned in toward Jasper. "Tosser basically intimated that Ana here had done something to cause Lexa's death."

"What?" Jasper blurted, instantly turning red. "Are you serious?"

"It was nothing," Ariana said under her breath, not wanting to dwell on this particular subject for any longer than strictly necessary. "He's just upset."

"So is everyone else at this school!" Jasper shot back. "That doesn't give him the right to—"

He started to get up, but Ariana placed her hand atop his thigh and shoved him back down as hard as she could. "Jasper, please. I just want to drop this. Let's not do anything to distract from the election tonight, okay?"

"She's right. If you kick his sorry arse, he might get a sympathy vote," April said, tearing into a roll.

Ariana smirked. As much as she loved Jasper, she was pretty sure that superstar athlete Palmer Liriano would triumph in a fistfight. But April's confidence was a nice ego stroke for Jasper and it seemed to calm him down.

"Fine," he said, blowing out a sigh. "But now you *have* to win tonight."

"Oh, don't worry," April said, lifting her water glass. "I've been telling all the girls in S and G how Palmer's been treating Ana. I don't think there's a single female that isn't voting for her."

"Yeah?" Ariana asked hopefully. Her heart felt all warm and light.

Could this really happen? Could she really be the next president of Stone and Grave?

"Yes. You're definitely going to win," April said, tilting the glass toward Ariana in a toast. "And winning is the best revenge."

THE COUP

"We all know why we're here," April said, after calling the Stone and Grave meeting to order. "Before we get on with the meeting, you should all know that our current vice president, Brother Starbuck, has asked that, since I initiated the process, I run the elections."

April cast a sardonic look in Palmer's direction, and Ariana knew exactly what it was meant to convey. Already April believed that Palmer was unfit to be president of their chapter, but his inability or unwillingness to step up to the plate tonight had sealed it. Palmer, meanwhile, sat slumped against the wall, his jeans and sneakers sticking out from under his bunched-up black robe. He gazed into a candle flame off to his right, his expression blank, as if there was nothing and no one else in the room.

"But first, let's all take a moment of silence for our sister, Lexa Greene," April said. "Forever in our hearts."

"Forever in our hearts," the brotherhood responded as one.

Ariana stared down at the floor. Her heart pounded an excited, anticipatory beat, and she felt uncomfortably like she had to pee. As much as she wanted to honor Lexa, she needed to get on with the vote. Each slowly passing minute of the day had meant an uptick in her tension level. By the time she, Tahira, and Maria had set out from Privilege House to walk down to the Tombs together, she had felt like she could barely breathe. Even with April's complete confidence that she would win, Ariana felt as if the chips were stacked against her. With Lexa gone and Soomie still MIA, there were fewer girls than guys in Stone and Grave. Even if she did land every single female vote, it wouldn't be enough. She'd need at least three guys to win. She'd been doing the math over and over all evening, giving herself a stabbing headache in the process. Now, whatever the outcome, she just wanted to have it over with. She wanted to know.

And yes, she wanted to win.

"Thank you," April said. Around the room, dozens of faces lifted. "And now, I will read the list of nominees."

"Brother Starbuck, do you accept your nomination?" she asked.

All eyes in the room turned to Palmer. He nodded. A movement so minuscule Ariana wasn't sure if it was real or a trick of light.

"So noted," April said with a frustrated sigh. She made a mark in her notebook.

"Sister Portia, do you accept your nomination?" April asked.

Suddenly Palmer's head snapped up. His gaze found Ariana's in the circle, and he sat up straight, pushing himself away from the wall and toward the circle. Clearly, no one had told him that she was nominated. Ariana found his obvious shock highly gratifying.

"I do," she said clearly, her voice strong.

"Thank you," April said. She made her note, then looked around. "At this time, it is my duty to open up the floor to any last-minute nominations," she said. "Let me remind you of the gravity of this decision. Tonight we will elect the person who will be our president for the remainder of the school year." She made eye contact with each and every brother and sister in the circle, driving her message home. "You must choose the person you think best exemplifies the values of the Stone and Grave. The person you would like to have representing us to the alumni. Now. Are there any further nominations?"

Christian Thacker raised his hand.

"Yes, Brother Darcy?"

Ariana's heart was in her throat. Palmer looked betrayed. Christian was really going to nominate someone else? Now? What was he trying to do, give her a coronary?

"I nominate Brother Lear," Christian said.

"No." Conrad's voice filled the room so utterly, Ariana flinched. "I'm sorry, Brother Darcy, but trust me, I'm not the best person for the job right now." He shifted, pulling his legs up story style under his robe and casting a sidelong glance at Palmer.

Ariana's pulse grew shallow and quick. What did that look mean? Was he not running in order to throw his support behind Palmer? Or did he think that Palmer should withdraw his nomination as well, since they were both in mourning? Ariana swallowed hard, hoping it was the latter.

Please, please, please let Conrad be on my side, she thought suddenly. *With Conrad on my side, I really have a chance.*

"All right then," April said. "For those of you who are new to this, we have open voting in Stone and Grave. There are no secrets among the brotherhood. I will call each of your names and you will answer with the name of the person for whom you wish to vote."

Ariana gripped the sides of her robe with both hands. Open voting? So she'd know who voted for her and who didn't. She'd be able to keep track. Suddenly her pulse throbbed so loudly she could hardly hear herself think. What was she supposed to say at her turn? Should she vote for herself, or do the mature, valiant thing and vote for Palmer?

She stared at her former love from across the circle. His jaw was set in a babyish pout, his fists stuffed under his arms. She remembered the way he'd attacked her in the hospital, in front of everyone, and then again in the common room. She suddenly felt so disgusted that she wasn't certain she'd be able to utter his name if she tried. There was a good possibility she'd gag on it first.

"We start with the newest members so that they can't be influenced by the votes of their elders," April continued, looking at Jasper. "So let's begin. Brother Amory Blaine?"

Jasper cleared his throat. "Sister Portia."

Palmer stared flaming daggers across the circle at Jasper. Ariana was certain he had been counting on the male vote the same way she was counting on the female vote.

"Brother Oliver Twist?"

Adam averted his eyes from Palmer's, looking at the stone floor. He picked at a fraying thread on the hem of his robe.

"Sister Portia."

Palmer's angry exhalation was audible throughout the room. Ariana's heart soared. Even though Adam had seconded her nomination, she hadn't been certain that she'd win his vote. He and Palmer went way back, and Palmer was part of the reason Adam, a scholarship student, had bothered applying to Atherton-Pryce at all. Still, Ariana should have known Adam would vote his conscience. He'd always been a brave and honorable guy.

April made a note in her book, and Ariana started to feel like she already had this thing won. Two guys had voted for her. If all the girls stayed on her side and she got one more guy, that was all she'd need.

Landon was next. Seated next to Ariana, he suddenly became unnaturally still.

"Brother Pip?" April said.

"Brother Starbuck," he said clearly.

It was all Ariana could do to keep from glaring at him. She'd known she'd never win his vote, but for some reason, hearing it out loud felt like a betrayal.

"Sister Portia?" April said.

Ariana held her breath. She knew that voting for Palmer would be the honorable thing to do, especially with everyone listening, but this election might come down to one vote. She had no interest in losing this battle for herself.

"Sister Portia," she said, her voice firm.

Luckily, no one flinched. April moved on to Tahira, who voted for Ariana, then continued around the circle with the more seasoned members. As Maria had predicted, every single girl voted for Ariana. She kept a running tally on her hands, curling a finger on her right for each of her votes, on her left for each of Palmer's, then starting over again, trying to keep track of the five-vote increments in her mind. The whole way, they were dead even. Finally, the vote came to Rob Mellon. All day, Ariana had gone back and forth over Rob, wondering whether he would go against Palmer. His girlfriend, Tahira, had been the one to nominate Ariana, after all, but he was also one of Palmer's best friends.

"Brother Von Hardwigg?" April said.

Rob glanced over at Tahira, then away. "Brother Starbuck."

Damn, Ariana thought.

Only Maria, Conrad, Palmer, and April were left. That meant that only Conrad could save her. He and Palmer had always been friends. What if Lexa's death had bonded them, rather than torn them apart? What if their shared grief had solidified their brotherhood?

If it had, Ariana would lose. But she couldn't lose. The Stone and Grave presidency was huge. It would open up opportunities she could scarcely even imagine. If she could win this, she'd be set for life. She'd never have to worry about anything ever again. Her mouth was dry and clammy as the vote came to Maria.

"Sister Estell—"

"Sister Portia," Maria interjected, not letting April finish her name. The note was made. The vote came to Conrad. "Brother Lear?"

Ariana stared at Conrad. He clasped his hands together and rested his chin against them. His elbows wide on his knees, he leaned forward and let out a sigh.

Please say Sister Portia, please say Sister Portia, please say . . .

"I cast my vote for . . ." He paused and looked over at Palmer. Palmer gazed back confidently. Slowly, Ariana's heart sank. The guy code was too strong. Conrad was going to vote for Palmer. "Sister Portia," he said finally.

Jasper let out a whoop, and a few people laughed, while others twittered nervously. It seemed Ariana wasn't the only one keeping a running score. And as long as April voted for her, she'd just won Stone and Grave.

"Brother Starbuck?" April asked.

"Brother Starbuck," Palmer said through his teeth.

April made a note, then lifted her face from the book. "And I, Sister Miss Temple, cast my vote for Sister Portia. Which means . . . the new president of Stone and Grave is Sister Portia."

A grin lit Ariana's face as Tahira reached in for a hug. There was the briefest smattering of applause, but they were quickly cut off.

"You have to be kidding me!" Palmer blurted, standing. "She's a newbie! She just transferred here, for God's sake!" he shouted, throwing an arm out in Ariana's direction. "What the hell is wrong with you people?"

"Brother Starbuck!" April admonished.

Palmer turned the color of ripe grapes. His nostrils flared as he whirled around. "Screw this crap," he said. "I'm outta here."

As he crossed the circle, he unzipped his robe and let it flutter to the ground. The heavy metal doors slammed behind him so loudly, the reverberation seemed to go on for days. For a long moment, no one dared move.

"So, should we . . . um . . . celebrate?" Tahira said finally.

Everyone looked at Ariana. She bit her bottom lip. *They're looking to their president,* she realized with a start. *They're already looking to me.*

Quickly, she scrambled to her feet. "No. No celebration. It's still too soon. Let's meet back here on Tuesday, midnight. In the meantime, we should be mourning our friend."

There were nods of agreement around the room, but still most members—even the guys—stopped by to congratulate Ariana. It was all she could do to keep from shouting and singing and doing a happy dance. Because whatever she said to the group, she *did* feel like celebrating.

She, Ariana Osgood, was the president of the most exclusive secret society at one of the most prestigious private schools in the world.

Celebrating was the only logical thing to do.

SO WELL

"We do have a bit of a logistical nightmare," April said, hurrying to keep up with Ariana's long strides as the members of Stone and Grave made their way back up the hill to Privilege House. As always, they had left the Tombs in pairs, spaced five minutes apart, to avoid drawing attention as a crowd. Not that anyone was out and about at one a.m. on a frigid December morning, but still. There was always the possibility of a glance out a window, and the primary goal of any good secret society was to remain secret. Ariana had started out the door with Jasper on her arm, but April had insisted on accompanying her so they could talk about the transfer of power. Ariana would have to settle for seeing Jasper in the morning. Such were the sacrifices a president had to make. "Everything you'll need—the archives, the bylaws, the presidential pin . . . all of it is in Lexa's possession. We can't let her parents find it, so basically we're going to have to pillage her things before someone finally gets round to emptying her room."

"I'll take care of it," Ariana said with a nod. "I'll go first thing in the morning. Maria can help me sort through her stuff. She may even know where Lexa kept it all."

"Good. Everything else is always stored inside the Tombs for safe keeping, so that won't be a problem," April said. She took a few deep breaths. "Do you mind if we slow down? Cardio's not really my thing."

"Sorry," Ariana said, concentrating to slow her steps. "I walk fast when I'm excited." She realized her faux pas the moment the words escaped her lips. She wasn't supposed to be excited. She was supposed to be somber and serious and pensive.

April smiled, her blue eyes sparkling behind her glasses. She paused and turned to face Ariana.

"It *is* exciting, isn't it?" she said under her breath, glancing over her shoulder into the darkness. "I know we're still in mourning and all, but I just have to say . . . I'm quite proud of and impressed by your achievement, Ana, coming so early in your Stone and Grave career. And I'm happy that the presidency will be retained by a woman."

"Thank you," Ariana said, beaming. "I'm proud too, to be honest."

"As you should be."

A fierce wind whipped through the Privilege House towers, howling ominously.

"Now let's get inside before we catch our death," April said, hugging herself. Her face paled in the moonlight and she cringed. "Ugh. Sorry. Can't believe I said that."

"It's okay," Ariana said, starting ahead. "Let's go."

Inside, Privilege House was deserted, the security lights in the lobby glowing green over the hardwood floors. Ariana could hardly contain herself as the elevator whipped her and April toward the top of the girls' tower. April bid her good night at her floor and stepped out. The second the doors closed and she was finally alone, Ariana let out a joyful squeal. She danced around the small, square space giddily, until the doors slid open again. By then, she was perfectly composed, just in case anyone happened to be milling around.

But the hallways were silent. Ariana made her way back to her room, stepped inside, and closed the door behind her. For a moment, she was all triumphant smiles. But as she looked around her room, her sense of joy quickly deflated at the bare, depressing room with one side completely unoccupied, the other sparse as a Spartan's quarters.

Not exactly the stuff celebrations were made of.

Feeling suddenly lonely, Ariana trudged to her bed and sat on the edge, tugging her cashmere scarf from around her neck. It was so unfair, really. She was sure that when Lexa was elected president there had been a huge bash in her honor. But for Ariana, nothing. All because of circumstances beyond her control. This was a huge night for her, but when she looked back on it years from now, there would be no memories of smiling faces and congratulations, no souvenir champagne bottles or photos to cherish. There would be nothing but the memory of . . . this.

A light knock on her door startled her. Ariana jumped up and opened it. Jasper grabbed her hand.

"Madame President, it's an honor," he said with a mock-formal nod.

Ariana cracked a smile. "Thanks, Jasper."

"Okay, I know we're supposed to be grim as the grave right now, but I can't allow it," he said, grabbing her scarf out of her hand and looping it around her neck. "We need to celebrate."

Ariana smiled for real. Jasper knew her so well. "What did you have in mind?"

He took both her hands and tugged her out the door. "Just follow me."

HEAVEN AND HELL

"Are we going to the boathouse?" Ariana whispered breathlessly. The cold wind caught her words and whipped them away almost before she said them. Overhead, the moon glowed full and bright, its luminous reflection rippling in the icy surface of the Potomac as she and Jasper raced down the bank toward the water.

"Not exactly," he replied with a grin.

Together they lit upon the wooden patio surrounding the huge, gleaming oak boathouse where the crew team lifted weights, socialized, and worked on their racing shells. But instead of heading for the back door, Jasper turned his steps, crunching through the gravel that surrounded the building. Ariana followed, keeping an eye on her feet in the dim light. At the edge of the water, Jasper started along a broken, overgrown concrete path, heading north toward the glowing lights of Washington, D. C.

"Okay, *where* are we going?" Ariana whispered again, her heart pounding from both exertion and excitement.

Jasper looked over his shoulder at her, his eyes teasing. "Are you really going to make me say it?"

"Say what?" she asked, her brow crinkling.

"That 'that's for me to know and you to find out'?" he said. Then he rolled his eyes. "Good Lord, you *did* make me say it."

He took her hand in his and Ariana giggled. His fingers were cold and dry, but she didn't mind in the least. Jasper tugged her around a bend and suddenly another boathouse loomed into view. This one was clearly much older. The wood planks of its walls were weathered and cracked, and the shutters around the upper windows tilted at dangerous angles. Faded orange signs reading KEEP OUT! hung on the garagelike doors on the water, and one lower windowpane was cracked and had been taped over with cardboard. Altogether, it wasn't the most welcoming place.

"Let me guess," Ariana said. "The *old* boathouse."

"Very astute, Madame President," he replied, leading the way over to a side door.

Ariana giggled. "Stop calling me that."

"You love it," Jasper teased. He paused with his hand on the door handle. "See? You're blushing!"

Ariana lifted her fingers to her cheeks. "Oh, God. I am. I'm sorry."

"Don't be. It's endearing," Jasper said. He leaned in and gave her a lingering kiss on the lips. "And now, for your surprise party."

With a flourish and a loud creak, Jasper opened the door. Light poured out from inside, and Ariana took a hesitant step forward. What she saw took her breath away. Jasper had decorated the boathouse from floor to ceiling, corner to corner, with dozens of multicolored balloons. Strands of twinkling lights lined the walls, illuminating the entire space. In the center of the huge, airy room was a table, laden with tiered trays of sweets—chocolates and pastries and mini cakes and tarts. A banner across the far wall read CONGRATULATIONS, ANA! in big block letters.

"Jasper!" Ariana took a step into the room and twirled in a circle, taking it all in from every angle. "This is spectacular! When did you have time to do all this?"

Jasper closed the door behind him and unbuttoned his wool jacket. "I have my ways."

"Yes, I suppose you do," she said.

Jasper flung his jacket over one of the chairs at the table and spread his arms wide. "Voilà."

Ariana grinned. "What would you have done if I hadn't won?"

He crossed over to her and wrapped his arms around her waist. His blond hair was wind-tossed and his nose was red from the cold, but he was still the handsomest guy she'd ever seen. "Not possible."

She tilted her head. "Come on."

"All right." Jasper raised his hands. He walked over to the banner, tugged it down, and turned it around, holding it up by the ends so she could see. She held her hand over her mouth to cover a laugh. On the opposite side the banner read BETTER LUCK NEXT YEAR!

"You are ridiculously sweet," Ariana said, leaning forward to kiss his cheek.

Jasper lifted one shoulder. "I do what I can." He tossed the banner aside and pulled out a chair for her. "So? What's your pleasure?"

"Hmmm . . ." Ariana was so giddy as she took her seat, she could barely keep herself from laughing out loud. She tapped her chin with her fingertips as she considered her dessert options, then plucked a raspberry tart from the top tier of one of the displays and took a bite. Her whole mouth filled with juicy, ripe sweetness. "Omigod, Jasper. This is so good."

"Interesting choice," he replied as he sat across from her. "I always thought you were a chocolate lover."

"I'm an all-sweets lover," Ariana replied, flicking a crumb from her lip with the very tip of her tongue. "No discrimination."

Jasper grinned. "A glutton. I like it."

Ariana blushed and took another bite of the tart. The water lapped gently along the walls of the boathouse and the wind whipped against the windowpanes, but she felt cozy, warm, and content inside the colorful, glowing room with Jasper. As much as she would have relished an elaborate, jam-packed party, this was pretty perfect.

"So, Briana Leigh Covington, you've just been named President of Stone and Grave. What are you going to do now?" Jasper asked in a reporter's voice.

"I don't know. I think I'll research the local bylaws . . . see if there's anything that needs a second look," Ariana said, wiping some crumbs from her fingers with a napkin. "I'm definitely interested in learning about how new members are chosen to be tapped. I think that's an area that needs improvement."

Especially if they were willing to let people like Lillian Oswald in—a girl who didn't even have a past.

Jasper laughed, a big, booming sound, and Ariana paused. "What?"

"You're supposed to say 'I'm going to Disney World,'" he told her.

Ariana's eyes narrowed. "What? Why would I say that?"

Jasper laughed so hard now, he doubled over. "Because . . . you know . . . at the Super Bowl? They always ask the MVP . . . what are you going to do now? And he always says—"

"I'm going to Disney World?" Ariana interjected, baffled. "But why? Why would they all want to do the same thing?"

Jasper shook his head. "Forget it."

"I mean, Disney World is a garish, filthy playground for the unwashed masses of the universe. Why would someone as wealthy and successful as a Super Bowl winner want to—"

"Forget it," Jasper said with an exaggerated sigh. "Clearly you're not a pop culture maven."

Ariana tried to shove aside her embarrassment over being laughed at. She'd never before been ashamed of the fact that she didn't get every reality show reference or commercial quote bandied about by her friends. She had always felt superior, in fact, in the not-knowing. She had more important things to do with her time than waste hours pouring over *OK!* magazine and watching MTV.

"No. Clearly not," she replied.

Jasper picked up a chocolate-covered cherry from a bowl and

popped it into his mouth. "The Princeton admissions committee is going to love you."

Ariana's heart skipped a quick beat. Princeton. Attending the Ivy League school had been Ariana's dream since the dawn of time, and now that she'd been officially elected Stone and Grave president, she was one step closer to getting in.

"Where are you going to apply?" Ariana asked, reaching for a chocolate cupcake.

"I hear Cornell and Brown are the easiest of the Ivies, so I'm starting there," he said with a smirk.

Ariana smiled. When she and Jasper had first started to get to know each other, he'd professed his aspiration to a life of leisure. But a guy like him was expected to go to an Ivy League school. Apparently this was his way of finding a happy medium.

"But I'm also going to apply to Tulane and LSU," Jasper added. "Mama would be happy if I ended up close to home."

"So Princeton's off the list, then?" Ariana asked, trying to sound casual. She and Jasper were juniors, after all. Anything could happen between now and their freshman year of college. Still, if she had to choose right now, she'd want him to come with her.

"It was," he said casually, reaching for another cherry. He popped it in his mouth and slowly smiled, a smile that made her want to curl right up in his arms. "Until you came along."

HONOR HER MEMORY

"None of us could have imagined the level of tragedy that has befallen this campus in the last two months," Headmaster Jansen said, her voice ringing out through the otherwise silent chapel on Thursday morning. She wore a black pencil skirt with a matching jacket and a gray silk blouse, and for the first time since Ariana had arrived at Atherton-Pryce Hall, her dark skin was free of makeup. Her delicate hands shook as she rested them on either side of the podium and looked out at the crowd. The school had postponed Lexa's memorial service until after the holiday, and now the students and faculty seated in the pews were as still as stone, their eyes shiny with unshed tears. "Lexa Greene was one of our shining stars. She had an incredible future ahead of her. One can only wonder what could have happened to make her feel so desperate, to make her feel that there was no other way out."

Ariana gripped her arm and squeezed. *You're going to make it right,* she reminded herself. *You're going to make it right.*

"We may never know the answer to that question. But there is one thing of which I am certain," the headmaster said, pacing out from behind her podium. "Lexa would want us to continue on. She would want all of you to honor her memory by doing your best, fulfilling your dreams, and living your lives to the fullest. That's just who she was."

Shakily, Maria reached over for Ariana's hand. Ariana released her grip on her own arm so that she could grip her friend's fingers. Maria pressed her lips into a semblance of a grim smile, her eyes so wet they swam. For the tenth time that day, Ariana wondered where Soomie was and whether Palmer and Conrad were here somewhere. Had they returned to campus, or were they off somewhere, grieving their loss in private?

"Everyone, please bow your heads in a moment of silence for our friend, Lexa Greene."

A choked sob escaped Maria's throat. She was practically crushing Ariana's fingers. Ariana closed her eyes, and pictured Lexa's smiling face.

I'm going to kill Reed Brennan, Lex. I'm finally going to do it. I'm going to do it for you.

In Ariana's mind's eye, Lexa's smile broadened, and a sense of peace and certainty settled in over Ariana's shoulders. Wherever Lexa was, she was proud of Ariana's resolution. Wherever she was, she approved.

"Thank you," the headmaster said. "May she rest in peace."

Ariana lifted her head. It was all she could do to keep from smiling in satisfaction.

"Now, to the practical," Headmaster Jansen began in a more formal tone. "The school has hired a grief counselor who will be setting up a permanent office here on campus. The doctor will be available to all of you during the school day, and a hotline will be set up for after hours. The hotline number will be posted around campus and on the school's website. He is an awarded professional, highly regarded in his field, so please make use of his expertise whenever you feel the need to talk to someone outside your own circle. But also know that each of you will be *required* to speak to him at one point this week. Half hour sessions have been scheduled for all students. You will report to the administration building at your designated time. No exceptions."

Ariana glanced across the aisle at Jasper. He rolled his eyes. For the first time all morning, voices could be heard among the student population, and none of them sounded happy.

"I've asked him to attend this morning's services so that we can all welcome him to the Atherton-Pryce Hall community," Headmaster Jansen continued. "Students, faculty, I'd like to introduce to you, Dr. Victor Meloni."

Ariana's free hand gripped the end of the pew as the entire world seemed to tilt beneath her. The edges of her vision went dark, and all she could see was the man rising up from the front pew to a smattering of awkward applause. Ariana recognized every detail with vivid horror—his thinning hair, his elbow-patched blazer, his broad shoulders, his square jaw. His cheap rubber-soled shoes squeaked as he strode toward the podium. When he turned toward the chapel, he wore an affected, overly concerned, and falsely friendly smile. The smarm seeped off of him, puddling like green goo at his feet. Ariana sank so low in her seat, her butt hung off the edge.

This was not possible. Why him? Why now? How could this be happening to her?

"Ana! Ow. Loosen up," Maria whispered.

Ariana looked down at her hand, clasped around Maria's slim fingers. She thought she heard a slight crack.

"Sorry," she muttered, releasing her friend.

Maria shook her hand, and Ariana could see the distinct outlines of her own fingers, white against the pained red of Maria's skin.

"Thank you all for that warm welcome," Dr. Meloni said loudly.

The rumbling tone of his voice sent violent shivers through Ariana's core. Suddenly, she heard that very voice inside her mind, shouting at an unnatural decibel, as if he was holding a bullhorn to his lips in the center of her skull.

You are not capable of change. If you were ever to be released from this facility, I am categorically certain that you would kill again.

"Ana? Ana?"

She could see Maria's lips moving, could feel the hard bench behind her back, but she was not there. She was back in Meloni's office at the Brenda T., clinging to the arms of her uncomfortable chair, her pulse thrumming in her very ears.

So no, Miss Osgood, you are not getting out of here. Not today, not

*tomorrow, not five years from now. Or ten. Or twenty. Not as long as I'm
the one signing your chart.*

"Ana?" Maria said again.

Somewhere in the chapel, a heavy book hit the floor. Ariana
flinched. She took in a breath and coughed, sitting up straight as
Maria clung to her arm.

"Are you okay?" Tahira's voice chimed in, coming from behind.

"I have to get out of here," Ariana muttered, catching her breath.

"What? You can't just leave morning services," Tahira protested,
gazing up at her as Ariana rose from her pew. Ariana kept her back to
the podium as she gathered up her coat and bag.

"I need some air. I have to . . . I have to go."

"I'll come with you," Maria said, starting to get up.

"No," Ariana blurted, startling her. She could already feel people
starting to stare. Could feel Meloni's eyes boring into the back of her
neck as she stood in the aisle. "Sorry. I just . . . I'd like to be alone for
a little while."

"Okay," Tahira said. "But text us if you need anything."

"You're sure you're okay?" Maria asked.

"I'll be fine," Ariana said confidently.

*As soon as I put as much distance between myself and Meloni as pos-
sible,* she added silently. She cast a glance at a concerned Jasper, then
speed-walked down the aisle. *I'll be okay as soon as I'm by myself and
have some time to think.*

"Rest assured that I'm here for all of you, whenever you need me,"
Dr. Meloni was saying, as Ariana reached the exit. "I've helped heal

hundreds of troubled souls in the past, and I'm looking forward to helping all of you."

Ariana shoved open the door, stepped out into the frigid, gray morning, and started to run.

IF NOT FOR HER

Back in her room, Ariana frantically, illogically shoved her desk chair against her door, then sat down on her bed, clutching at the sheets. Her throat closed over and she choked out a sob. She glanced around her room frantically, as if there were answers among the neatly organized books, the labeled boxes of shoes in her open closet, the art and travel posters tacked to the walls at perfect right angles.

What am I going to do? What am I going to do?

Meloni was here. He had invaded her carefully constructed, perfect new life. He was here and she was going to have to see him. The headmaster had made that crystal clear. She was going to have to attend her mandatory grief-counseling appointment, and if she did that, she'd be headed right back to the Brenda T. before she could say the words "electric chair." Ariana's stomach clenched suddenly and she doubled over.

*This can't be happening. This can*not *be happening.*

On her knees on the cold wood floor of her dorm room, the walls seemed to close slowly in on her. It wasn't real. It wasn't possible. How could he have found her?

She covered her face with her hands and wailed at the injustice of it all. There was nothing in the world but her anger, her pain. Nothing in the world but this white-hot fear inside her chest. She had worked so hard, sacrificed so much, done unspeakable things in the name of self-preservation, and for what? So that cocky jackass could waltz on in here and take it all away from her?

Ariana lifted her tear-stained face. The first thing her eyes fell upon was the folded newspaper sticking out of the outer pocket on her messenger bag.

GEORGETOWN SOCCER STAR, were the only words she saw.

"No," Ariana blurted.

She whipped the newspaper out of her bag and found Reed's name buried inside the article.

"It's *you!*" she spat through clenched teeth, crushing the newspaper in her palm. "It's *your* fault. *You're* the reason I'm here. *You're* the reason all of this had to happen." She pushed herself to her feet, focusing all her ire, all her grief, everything inside of her, on the ball of newsprint. "If it wasn't for you, I would have graduated from Easton and I'd be at Princeton right now. If it wasn't for you I never would have *met* Victor Meloni. Thomas would still be alive. Briana Leigh would still be alive. *You* killed them! You sent me to that fucking prison and you unleashed Kaitlynn Nottingham on the world. Brigit died because of you. Lexa died because of you. Every last ounce of their blood is on *your* pretty little stupid fucking head!"

Ariana whipped around and drove the fist holding the newspaper into the wall as hard as she possibly could.

Her hand exploded in pain. The skin on her knuckles cracked open and her fingers burned. But still, it wasn't enough. Letting out a screech of rage, Ariana tore the posters from the wall above her bed and ripped them to shreds. She picked up her makeup mirror and hurled it across the room like a Frisbee, shattering it into a billion glittering shards. Nothing was safe from her path. She tore her designer clothes from their silk hangers, threw her computer to the floor, ripped the curtains free of their rods. She shredded and smashed and slammed and screamed until nothing in the room was left intact.

And then, chest heaving, she sank to the floor and curled into a ball on her side, pressing her forehead into her knees. Reed's eyes, Meloni's smirk, Reed's grin, Meloni's condescending sneer. The images flashed through her mind, rapid-fire, melding and melting and contorting into a frightening, ghoulish mask. Ariana grabbed at her hair, shook her head violently, willed her enemies out of her mind—out of existence.

Breathe, Ariana. Just breathe.

In, one . . . two . . . three . . .

Out, one . . . two . . . three . . .

In, one . . . two . . . three . . .

Out, one . . . two . . . three . . .

In, one . . . two . . . three . . .

Out, one . . . two . . . three . . .

In, one . . . two . . . three . . .

Out, one . . . two . . . three . . .

Soon, her pulse started to calm. Her breathing returned to normal. Her brain began to clear. Soon all that was left behind was a simple, rhythmic beat.

She must die . . . he must die . . . she must die . . . he must die . . .

Suddenly there was a polite, but firm knock on her door. Ariana sat up, heart in her throat, pressing her fingertips into the floor. Meloni. It had to be. He'd seen her and now he had come here to take her back to jail. Ariana stood up quickly and whirled around, searching the room for a weapon, but there was too much destruction, too much chaos. She brought her hands to her temples and pressed.

This was it. This was it. This was the end.

"Ana? It's me. Palmer."

Ariana froze. She could feel her heartbeat in her cheeks, radiating heat throughout the room. What the hell was Palmer doing here? She made a move for the door, feeling suddenly silly and overly dramatic when she saw the back of her chair shoved up under the door handle. She tugged it out and pushed it against the wall, then opened the door just a crack.

"Oh, hey," Palmer said, as if surprised she was there.

"Hey," Ariana responded. She opened the door a bit wider, wedging her body between the door and the wall, to block his view of the mess behind her.

"Listen, I'm sorry for the way I've been acting . . . ," Palmer said unexpectedly. There was a slam somewhere in the hallway and he looked around. "I really need to talk to you. Can I come in?"

Instead of waiting for an answer, Palmer laid his hand flat against the door and slipped past her. Ariana didn't even have a chance to say a word or hold up a hand to stop him. The second he was over the threshold, his jaw went slack. Ariana stood there with her arms around her waist and watched him. She watched him take in the torn posters, the shredded books, the broken glass. He nudged a pile of rumpled clothing and cracked frames and computer wires with his foot. As he turned, ever so slowly, in a baffled circle, Ariana quietly closed her door.

"What the hell did you do?" Palmer demanded finally.

"I just . . . I guess I kind of lost it," Ariana said, her brow furrowed.

"Lost it? Are you serious? This goes way past 'lost it,' Ana." He brought his hand to his forehead. "My God. You really are insane. I mean, this is not normal. This is not the kind of thing a normal person does."

"Shut up," Ariana snapped.

"Shut up? Are you serious?" He looked her up and down like she was yesterday's rotting trash. "I can't believe I came over here to apologize to you. You're completely out of your mind! Honestly? I'm starting to wonder if you really did do something to cause Lexa's death."

Ariana arms uncurled and her fingers clenched into fists at her sides. Suddenly the four walls around her began to close in, crowding her out, making it impossible to breathe. All she could see was Palmer's face. His awful, unforgiving, accusing face. And all she wanted to do was tear it off his over-inflated head.

"Why are you just standing there?" Palmer spat. "Say something, you certifiable freak."

Ariana knew he was in pain. She knew that being in mourning could screw with a person and make him act like a jerk. But she had never imagined that calm, collected, mature Palmer Liriano could be so outright cruel. Suddenly she saw herself reeling back and hitting him. She saw herself picking up her desk chair with both hands and swinging as hard as she could. She saw herself screeching at the top of her lungs and rushing him so hard, so fast, and so unexpectedly that he lost his balance and went flying through the windowpane, shedding broken glass all over the grass below and falling to his bone-crushing, skull-cracking death.

But she couldn't do any of that. Of course she couldn't. There had been too many deaths already, and all inside her circle of friends. If Palmer were to die right in her own room, the questions would certainly start.

Breathe, Ariana. Just breathe.

In, one . . . two . . . three . . .

Out, one . . . two . . . three . . .

"You know what, Palmer? I *do* have something to say," she told him, turning toward the door again. Her palm was so sweaty it slipped once on the knob before she was able to grip it and get the door open. "Get out."

Palmer scoffed, shaking his head in a condescending way. But he did walk by her, and paused in the doorway. He made a little teepee with his hands and placed it in front of his mouth for a moment, smiling mirthfully the whole time.

"Thank God we broke up," he said, looking her in the eye. "And here's fair warning: I am going to make sure that every single person in Stone and Grave knows exactly what kind of psychopath they've elected as their president. Enjoy your power trip while it lasts, Ana. Your days are numbered."

Then, with one last derisive glance, he turned on his heel and walked away. Ariana had never slammed a door so hard in her life.

PEACE OF MIND

Ariana clutched the steering wheel as she searched the crowded downtown streets for an open space. She realized too late that she had just passed one and slammed on her brakes. The guy behind her honked his horn and swerved, but Ariana ignored both him and the rude gesture he tossed her way. Gritting her teeth, she quickly and deftly swung her car into the parallel spot.

"Okay, you're here. Just calm down. Palmer can't really hurt you. Anything he tells anyone will be hearsay. Everything's going to be fine."

Ariana glanced in the mirror, taking a deep, soothing breath. Before leaving campus, she had meticulously straightened her room, making sure there was no shred of evidence of her freak-out left behind. Then she had shoved the pieces of her current disguise into her leather Louis Vuitton satchel and hit the road. All morning she had been running errands and steering clear of Atherton-Pryce, all the better to avoid the honorable Dr. Victor Meloni. But now, she'd made it to her final stop of the day.

With a discerning eye, Ariana scrutinized her look from all angles. Her blond wig was fashioned into a ponytail, which stuck out through the hole in the back of the battered Washington Nationals baseball cap Palmer had once left in her room. Her black wool peacoat was the blandest she owned, and she'd decided on jeans and sneakers to complete her girl-next-door look. Altogether, she appeared pretty darn forgettable.

"This is just in case," she told herself firmly. "You always need to have a plan B."

She smoothed the ponytail, got out of the car, and walked toward the marble-columned building across the street. Inside the bank, the atmosphere was hushed and professional. The brown granite floors gleamed, and the security guard took no notice of her as she crossed to the customer service desk.

"Can I help you?" the woman behind the counter asked, looking up with a smile. Her makeup was about three shades darker than the skin on her neck, and it was all Ariana could do to keep from cringing.

"Yes, I'd like to open a new account," she replied, averting her eyes to keep from staring.

"Of course. Mr. Lawrence can help you with that."

She indicated a nearby desk where an elderly gentleman sat in front of a glowing computer screen, his red tie adorned with candy canes.

Perfect, Ariana thought. *This guy will be eating out of my palm.* And at least she wouldn't have to deal with staring at that line for the next fifteen minutes.

"Hello!" Mr. Lawrence said, standing as she approached. "So you'd like to open an account with us Miss . . . ?"

"Walsh. Emma Walsh," Ariana said.

"All right, Miss Walsh, have a seat. I'll just need to see a driver's license and one other form of ID."

Ariana produced her wallet from her bag and fished her Emma Walsh license from the window pocket. Then she took out her passport and laid that out for him as well. Mr. Lawrence hummed Christmas carols to himself while he inputted her information, using the address on the license.

"Okay, and your telephone number?" he asked.

Ariana recited the number from the new cell phone she'd just procured for herself at the mall that morning—the same mall where she'd purchased the wig. Mr. Lawrence's pudgy fingers flew over the keys.

"All righty. Now. We have many different types of accounts," he said, pushing his desk blotter toward her. On it were three large squares, one white, one blue, and one gold, each advertising the different levels of accounts and how much money was needed to open each. "Were you interested in checking . . . savings . . . ?"

"Well, my grandmother wanted me to put most of it in savings, as long as it was linked to a checking account so I could access it if I needed it."

Ariana made sure her hands shook as she withdrew the crumpled check from her bag.

"Your grandmother?" he asked.

"Yes, she . . . she wrote me this check before she . . . passed away."

Ariana brought her free hand to her face, covering both her mouth and her nose.

"Oh! I'm so sorry!" Mr. Lawrence snatched a tissue out of a box on his desk and handed it to her. "Was this recent?"

Ariana nodded, pressing the tissue to her nose. "A few days ago."

She laid the check on his desk and flattened it with both hands. She had actually written it out to herself that morning, then let it sit, crumpled, in the bottom of her bag so it would be good and battered when she arrived at the bank. Mr. Lawrence did a double take when he saw the huge amount. He cleared his throat and smoothed his tie.

"Well. I'd say you definitely qualify for our gold-level accounts," he said. "Which is perfect because you'll be able to transfer money to and from your checking without paying a fee, provided your total combined balance remains above fifty thousand dollars." He glanced at the check again. "Which . . . I don't think you'll have any problem with."

"Okay," Ariana said tearfully. "That sounds good."

"What do you say we put the bulk of it in high-yield savings, and . . . let's see . . . would twenty thousand be okay in the checking?"

His voice cracked a bit on the "twenty" and his smile twitched. Ariana had a feeling he was thinking about how he'd never see this much money in his lifetime, yet here she was, a teenager, rolling in it already. Such was life, Mr. L.

"Better make it fifty," Ariana replied, touching the tissue to the corners of her eyes. "I think that's what Grandma Covington said."

"Okay," he replied with a nod. "Fifty it is." He tapped away at the keyboard, then opened a drawer to remove two separate deposit slips. "You'll just need to fill these out and sign them, and we'll be all set to open those accounts and issue you an ATM card."

"Great," Ariana replied.

"If you don't mind, Miss Walsh, I'd like to call my manager over and introduce her to you. She likes to meet all of our new and . . . esteemed account holders personally."

And by esteemed you mean filthy rich, Ariana thought.

"No, I'd rather not," Ariana said, knowing that the fewer people who remembered her here after today, the better off she'd be. "I'm not really up to it . . . right now . . ." She forced herself to dissolve into tears and covered her whole face with the tissue.

"No, no. Of course not. That's quite all right," Mr. Lawrence said, reaching over to pat her arm. "Please don't cry. You can meet her the next time you come in. Would that be preferable?"

Ariana sniffled hugely. "Next time. Perfect."

Of course, there wouldn't be a next time. If she did have to leave the country, she'd never set foot in this branch again. And if she didn't have to leave, she intended to keep this account open and full as an emergency fund for as long as she felt she needed it.

"Thank you so much for your help, Mr. Lawrence," Ariana said as she signed the deposit slips with a flourish.

"Of course, my dear. Of course." He slid the check and the deposit slips into his hand and arose from his chair. "I just need to take these over to a teller to make the deposits. I'll be right back."

"Thank you."

As Mr. Lawrence scurried off, headed for the long cashiers' desk at the back of the bank, Ariana took a deep breath and looked around. The bank's motto was emblazoned across practically everything in sight, from the desk blotter to the letterhead to the front window.

International Trust. For your peace of mind.

Ariana smiled. For her peace of mind indeed.

THERAPIST PAST

Ariana walked to dinner that night between Tahira and Maria, her face hidden under huge Donna Karan sunglasses, a wool hat pulled low over her ears, the collar of her black coat turned up over her cheeks. All she could think about was getting into the dining hall and off the open quad. Dr. Meloni had never once eaten the cafeteria food at the Brenda T., preferring to order in his meals from overly expensive gourmet restaurants and eat them in the privacy of his office. She could only hope his snobbish culinary tendencies would continue during his tenure at Atherton-Pryce.

"Okay, what's up with the sunglasses at night?" Tahira asked Ariana, her brow creased with what could only be serious fashion concern.

Luckily, Ariana had long since prepared for the question. "I've had a splitting headache all day. I can hardly even look at a light," she explained. "These seem to help."

"Well, just don't let it become a thing," Tahira said, holding the collar of her fur jacket closed over her throat.

"She's right," Maria chimed in. "People will start to think your success has turned you eccentric, and eccentricity is frowned upon around here."

"Point taken," Ariana replied.

She looked up at the dining hall door, wishing she could just make a run for it. But, she supposed, that would also be rather eccentric behavior. She had to try to keep that kind of thing to a minimum, especially now that Palmer was apparently bent on making her out to be a loon to all their friends. For a moment, she considered asking Maria and Tahira if he'd said anything to them today, or if they'd heard anything via the APH gossip mill, but she decided against it. Asking about a rumor only gave it credence.

"So have either of you guys heard from Soomie?" Tahira asked, her breath making steam clouds in the cold air.

Ariana shook her head. "Not a word."

"Let's all call her right now," Maria suggested, pausing to take her phone out of her bag.

Ariana stopped two steps ahead. "I've already called her twice today. Can't we just get inside?"

"If it goes to voice mail like it always does, it'll only take two seconds," Maria told her, hitting a speed-dial button and lifting the phone to her ear. "I just don't want her thinking anyone's forgotten about her."

Ariana clucked her tongue impatiently, which her friends didn't seem to notice, and hugged her own arms as she waited.

"Voice mail," Maria said, rolling her eyes. "Hey, Soomie. It's Maria," she said into the phone. "I'm here with Ana and Tahira and we're just . . . we just want to talk to you. We want to know you're okay. And we also wanted to tell you . . . hang in there. It's going to get better. I promise. If there's anything we can do, please, just . . . call us back."

She ended the call and shoved the phone away.

"God. Where could she possibly be?" Tahira mused, pushing her hands into her pockets.

"I just don't get it," Maria said, tilting her head back and blowing a cloud of steam toward the sky.

"I know," Ariana chimed in, glancing over her shoulder at the dining hall. "You'd think her parents would at least call us and let us know where she is. Don't they realize there are people here who care about their—"

The words died on her tongue as a dog's bark, loud and persistent, filled the air. Suddenly the entire world constricted to a tiny, solid, pinprick. Walking past them, not three yards away, were Dr. Meloni and his trusty dog, Rambo. The dog strained on his leash, lurching in her direction, as if he recognized her scent. Ariana turned away from the dog, but she could hear Dr. Meloni coaxing the Doberman under his breath, cooing to him to behave.

"Come on, Rambo. Come on, boy. You know better than that."

As he passed, he shot a glance at Ariana and her friends. Ariana's knees went weak. She sidestepped slightly, angling so that her face wouldn't be visible past Maria's shoulder.

"Ana? Are you okay?" Maria asked, reaching for her. "You look like you're gonna pass out."

"Are you having another . . . episode?" Tahira asked under her breath.

Ariana shook her head, but couldn't formulate an answer. Episode? Her friends thought she was having episodes? This was so not good. And if Palmer *had* said anything . . . well, then that was even worse. Dr. Meloni and Rambo kept moving away, headed slowly toward the Administration Building, but even with the distance between them, Ariana couldn't seem to make herself breathe.

"Ana?" Maria said.

Tahira gripped her arm. "Ana? You're turning purple."

Come on, Ariana. Just breathe! But he's here. He's right there. He's going to destroy me.

Ariana doubled over, bracing her hands above her knees.

"Omigod! She's not breathing," Maria said. "We have to get a doctor."

I have to run. I have to get the hell out of here. I have to . . . to . . . to run!

Her mind started to fog over. Her brain floated in space. She was going to faint. If she didn't get some oxygen soon, she was done for.

Breathe, Ariana. Just breathe.

"I'm going inside," Tahira said. "I'll grab the nurse! Or that new shrink. Shrinks know CPR, right?"

"No!" the word growled out of Ariana's throat. Tahira froze.

Breathe, Ariana. Just breathe.

Ariana closed her eyes, concentrated as hard as she could, and sucked in a breath.

In, one . . . two . . . three . . .

Out, one . . . two . . . three . . .

In, one . . . two . . . three . . .

Out, one . . . two . . . three . . .

Tahira placed her hand on Ariana's back in a comforting way, holding it there until she was finally able to stand up straight again. Until she was finally able to see clearly.

"God, Ana. Are you all right?" Maria asked, looking terrified.

"Everything all right over there, ladies?" Meloni called out.

"Tell him I'm fine," Ariana said through clenched teeth.

"But you're—"

"Tell him!" she hissed.

"We're fine!" Tahira shouted shrilly.

"All right then. Better get inside. It's going to be below zero tonight," he replied.

"We will. Thank you," Maria called out. She put her arm around Ariana's shoulder. "Are you okay?"

"I'm fine," Ariana said. "I don't . . . I don't know what happened."

"Looked like a panic attack to me," Tahira said. "My brother used to have them . . . pretty much any time my father was in the room."

Maria managed to laugh. "You should have let us call him over," she said, glancing at Meloni's retreating back. "He could've helped."

"Like I said, I'm fine," Ariana said, staring past her friend at her worst enemy.

He's here. He's here on campus. He's found me. The one person who could send me right back to the Brenda T. He's here. He's here. He's here.

"You know what? I think I'm going to skip dinner," she said.

"Are you sure?" Maria asked.

"Yeah. I kind of just want to go for a walk," Ariana said. She backed up the pathway toward Privilege House. All she could think about was getting away. "Maybe bring me something back at the dorm when you're done?"

"Sure," Tahira said. "We'll try to eat fast."

"Thanks, guys," Ariana said, attempting to smile, to put them at ease. Then she turned on her heel and speed-walked off, headed for the safety of her private room. But even as her pulse began to normalize, she realized she wouldn't be able to hide forever. And she couldn't keep having panic attacks in front of her friends, especially not with Palmer out to ruin her. Sooner or later she was going to have to figure out a way to deal with this. Sooner or later either she or Meloni was going to have to go.

PSYCHIC

Why did he have to show up now? That was what was so unfair about this whole Meloni situation. Just when Ariana had gotten together her plan for Reed Brennan, just when she was on the verge of executing the bitch that had ruined her life, Victor Meloni had to waltz in and distract her. Why couldn't he have just come next week when Reed would already be dead and buried? When she'd have all kinds of time to work the problem? Why couldn't she just for once catch a break?

Ariana got up from her desk chair and began to pace.

Victor Meloni had to die. That was the only solution. Even if he was fired, even if he left campus, Ariana would always be looking over her shoulder, always be wondering when and where he was going to pop up next. She simply could not have an enemy like him out there walking the streets, moving in her circles. He had to go. He just had to go.

But how?

Ariana's stomach grumbled with hunger, her face felt tight and dry from exhaustion and the cold, and her head pounded with pain after her panic attack, but she ignored it all. She needed to figure out the best way to deal with Meloni, and she needed to do it fast.

The idea of a gun was very satisfying. Everyone else had died so cleanly. Knocked over the head or drowned in a lake or lying in a hospital bed. But Meloni . . . Meloni was special. He was truly evil. He deserved a seriously messy death. Ariana paused in the center of her room, her heart skipping an excited beat. A gun, yes. But how was she to get one? And if she did get one, wouldn't they be able to trace it back to her?

She gnawed on the side of her thumb, narrowing her eyes as she executed a slow twirl on her throw rug. Maybe . . . maybe she didn't need one. Dr. Meloni had to have a gun of his own. He was just that type of guy. He had worked for years inside a facility for the criminally insane. Of course he'd bought a gun to protect himself lest any of his former patients or their family members ever come calling. He was just that narcissistic. Just that self-important. To think that someone would one day seek him out for revenge.

Ariana pressed her hands together. She had to get inside Meloni's house and do some recon. And she had to do it soon. Before she bumped into him one day on campus, or worse—before her mandatory meeting was scheduled.

A sudden rap on the door stopped her heart. Ariana's blood ran cold. What if Tahira or Maria had ignored her request and told Dr. Meloni that their friend was sick? What if he'd come up here to make sure she was all right? Could she hide in the closet? Pretend not to be here?

"I know you're in there!" Jasper's voice teased through the door.

Everything inside of Ariana relaxed. She lunged for the door and pulled him inside, closing it firmly behind him.

"Hey," he said with a smile. He kissed her quickly, his lips freezing cold and dry. "You must be psychic."

"What? Why?" Ariana asked.

"I got us dinner," he said, dropping a takeout bag on her desk. He shook his jacket off his shoulders and tossed it on Kaitlynn's bare bed. "When I went to the dining hall to get you and saw that you weren't there, I figured you had some kind of premonition that you shouldn't fill up on greasy roast beef when I was going to show up bearing gourmet Chinese."

Ariana inhaled the sweet and spicy scents wafting her way from the open bag. Never could she have imagined that she would feel so grateful to someone for bringing her spring rolls and rice. Clearly, he was the one who was psychic. He seemed to always know exactly what she needed.

"You might be the greatest boyfriend of all time," she said.

Jasper slipped his arm around her waist and smiled. "I aim to please."

Then he kissed her, and for the first time all day, Ariana forgot all about Victor Meloni. She forgot all about Reed and Palmer and what tomorrow might bring. All that mattered was where she was right at that very moment.

With Jasper.

FORMER LIFE

The sun was just starting to brighten the gray morning sky when Ariana slipped into the Georgetown biology building's admittedly dungeonlike basement through a service entrance in the back. The hallway smelled of formaldehyde and rotting garbage, and she covered her nose with her cashmere scarf to keep from choking. Taking a deep breath through her mouth, she stood for a moment and listened. All was silent and dim. The only real light in the underground hallway emanated from the glowing, red exit sign behind her head.

Somewhere in this basement was Reed Brennan, and wherever she was, she was all alone. Adrenaline coursed through Ariana's veins, and her fingers curled into claws. She couldn't wait to sink her fingernails into the bitch's skin.

Walking on her tiptoes, Ariana crept to the first door and peeked through the long, skinny window. The room was dark. She checked the lab across the hall. One light shone at the professor's desk, but it appeared to have been left on overnight. There was no sign of life. Outside the third door, Ariana hit pay dirt. There was a clipboard tacked to the wall, displaying a lab schedule. Under SIX O'CLOCK, FRIDAY MORNING, Reed Brennan—and only Reed Brennan—had signed her name.

Suddenly, there was a loud click—the sound of a bolt lock opening—and Ariana heard the upstairs door creak. It had to be Reed. She was five minutes late, but she was here. Heart in her throat, Ariana flung herself inside the lab and pressed back against the cinderblock wall. The only windows in the long, dank room, were set high in the opposite wall, and all were closed against the cold.

All the better to keep anyone from hearing you scream, Ariana thought, smiling in anticipation.

All the overhead lights were off, making it nearly pitch dark.

All the better to surprise you, Ariana added.

She heard shuffling on the stairs and bit down hard on her lip to keep from laughing with sheer glee. But then, she heard a voice. And it wasn't Reed's.

"Can't believe you made me get up at the ass crack of dawn. Have I *ever* been a morning person?"

The triumphant excitement emanating from Ariana's heart froze in midair and shattered. It was Noelle Lange.

"I can't believe you actually came," Reed replied.

"Wait. I had a choice?" Noelle said.

Ariana's heart was in turmoil. She hadn't laid eyes on Noelle Lange since her sham of a funeral last summer. What was she doing here?

Did she go to Georgetown too? But no. This was not possible. If Noelle were a student here Ariana undoubtedly would have seen her by now. And Noelle had always dreamed of going to Yale. There was no doubt in Ariana's mind that she had found a way to get there. This made no sense. No sense at all.

"I already e-mailed the professor to tell him I wouldn't be in class because of the memorial service," Reed said. "I just have to print out the lab I finished last night and then we can get out of here."

"Fine. And then you *are* buying me one huge cup of coffee," Noelle chided.

They were right outside the door. Ariana looked around in desperation. She dropped down behind the first storage table and yanked on the cabinet door, but it was full of beakers and Bunsen burners. The doorknob began to turn. Ariana whirled around and spotted a four-doored closet. Praying it wasn't locked, she pulled on the handle. It swung open, dumping several lab coats onto the floor and all over her feet. Ariana scooped them up in her arms, jumped inside, and swung the door closed behind her, jamming her fingers in the process. The pain exploded so suddenly she saw stars.

"Damn it," she hissed under her breath.

She brought her fingers to her mouth and sucked on them, half to dull the pain and half to keep herself quiet. The lights in the lab flickered to life and Ariana could just see a sliver of the room as Noelle and Reed entered. She caught a glimpse of Noelle's long, dark hair as she passed the closet and paused. Her black coat. Her diamond earrings. Her heart felt as if it was going to burst with longing.

Noelle. Noelle was right there. If Ariana reached out she could have grabbed her sleeve.

Suddenly, her vision started to prickle over. She leaned back against the hooks full of lab coats behind her, closed her eyes and breathed.

In, one . . . two . . . three . . .

Out, one . . . two . . . three . . .

"I can't believe we have to fly to Texas for this," Noelle lamented, dropping onto a tall lab stool. "Doesn't Kiran's mom know that she lived for New York? If she's going to be memorialized, it should be there."

"She wants to do it at home, where Kiran grew up. I get that," Reed said.

Ariana heard a printer whir to life.

"Just so you know, my mom's going to be there, and I'm sure she's going to badger you about coming to St. Barth's this year."

Ariana's arms curled tighter around the stack of musty lab coats in her arms. St. Barth's. So the Easton crowd was still spending Christmas down there. And now, Reed was a part of it. Reed had probably met Upton Giles and Poppy Simon and the Hathaways. She had probably spent Christmas morning at Noelle's with all the families. She was really one of them now. And Ariana was not.

Hot fury began to bubble in Ariana's veins. This was so unfair. She was supposed to be killing Reed right now. Strangling every last breath out of her. Experiencing the most perfect moment of her life. But instead she was forced to listen to *this*.

"I'll just tell her the same thing I told her last time," Reed said.

"Thanks for the invitation, but me and St. Barth's do not mix."

Noelle laughed lightly. "She can't argue with that."

"No one could," Reed replied. "Besides, Scott is going to Vail with his new girlfriend and Josh invited me to see his parents' house in Vienna. So I'll be spending Christmas in Croton, and then jetting to the *Continent* for a week before going back to the Cape for New Year's."

She put on a snotty voice on the word "Continent," as if calling Europe that was some kind of joke. Ariana gritted her teeth. Reed would never set foot on the Continent if she had anything to say about it.

"God. Who knew you were going to become such a jet-setter?" Noelle said.

"I know, right?" Reed replied with a grating laugh. "Okay. I'm all set. Let's get out of here."

"Finally," Noelle said in a dramatic way.

Ariana pressed back against the wall as first Reed's coat, then Noelle's, flashed by the sliver of open space between the two doors.

Ariana's pulse stopped. Noelle was leaving. It was so unfair. She was supposed to be Ariana's best friend for life, not Reed's. For a fleeting moment, she wondered what Noelle would do if she revealed herself to her. Would she be happy to see her? Relieved to find her alive and well? Would she throw her arms around her and hug her and invite *her* to St. Barth's for the holiday?

It was a lovely fantasy. But as Reed doused the lights and the two of them stepped out, Ariana knew it could never come true. She could never reveal herself to anyone from her old life. Not even Noelle. Suddenly her heart hurt with a severity she had never imagined before. It was so wrong, that Reed got to be with Noelle—got to laugh with her, know her secrets, go on trips with her. Noelle had been Ariana's best friend first. Ariana's confidante. She was just one more of the many things Reed had stolen out from under her. Just another reason Reed deserved to die.

The lab door closed and their footsteps faded away. Ariana held her breath, counted to one hundred, then shoved open the closet doors. Her body felt as if it weighed five hundred pounds, most of the suffocating bulk concentrated in her chest. She let the lab coats slip to the floor as angry, disappointed tears filled her eyes.

She had come here to finally end Reed. Finally end all the misery and suffering. Finally win justice for all of those who had died. But she had been thwarted by her own best friend. Why did these things keep happening to her? Why couldn't she catch a break? Why couldn't she, for once, get what she deserved?

THE OBLIGATORY ENTOURAGE

"Here's your latte and cinnamon scone, Ana." Quinn placed the cup and plate on the marble table in front of Ariana on Saturday morning and stood back with a smile, smoothing her long, strawberry blond hair over one shoulder. Jessica hovered there as well, ready to take orders. Ariana looked at her eager face and decided to throw her a bone. "It's chilly in here this morning, isn't it?" she said, glancing around as if looking for an open window or some other source of the cold.

"Do you want me to get you a sweater?" Jessica asked, rising onto her toes.

"That would be fabulous," Ariana replied. "The gray cashmere, I think."

"I'll be right back." And just like that, Jessica was gone, a blur of black curls and blue skirt.

"Anything else I can get you?" Quinn asked. "Otherwise I have a study session for my econ exam this morning."

"No, thank you, Quinn. You're dismissed." Ariana gave a quick wave of her hand to punctuate the statement.

"Okay. Text me if you need anything. Anything at all," Quinn said as she gathered her things.

"Oh, I will."

Ariana smiled to herself as Quinn hurried off. There was no better way to overcome a serious failure than to spend a morning being waited on by a team of servants anticipating her every need. When she'd woken up this morning, part of her had wanted to just stay in bed and wallow over her crash and burn at Georgetown, but she had forced herself to get up and go out into the world—to remind herself of the things she had to live for. Like the perks of being Stone and Grave president. Over the past two days, Ariana had received dozens of congratulatory phone calls from prestigious alumni, and gifts had started to pour in from all corners of the globe. Sitting next to her plate right now was a stack of invitations that had arrived in her mailbox just that morning, everything from an invite to a charity event at the botanical gardens, given by a prestigious Stone and Grave alum, to a request for her presence at a luncheon at the Capitol, to a ticket to the New Year's Eve MTV bash in New York City. Ariana smiled just looking at them. Briana Leigh Covington really was a star.

A star who can't even execute the simplest plan, a little voice inside her mind chided.

Ariana's heart sank as the memory of how very close she'd come to being caught yesterday came flashing back in vivid relief. She placed her coffee cup down and gritted her teeth. Why couldn't Reed have been there alone, like she'd said she was going to be? Why did everyone always have to be so damned unreliable? When Ariana said she was going to do something, she did it. How else were people supposed to make plans?

"It's just so infuriatingly impertinent," she muttered under her breath.

If Reed hadn't changed her schedule for the day at the last minute, she would be dead by now, and Ariana could get on with her life—get on with plotting her next move with Meloni and securing her future. But no. She had to go finishing her lab the night before. Even that wouldn't have been so bad, if she'd simply not shown up at all. Ariana would have waited for a while before giving up, going home, and coming back with a new plan. But that wasn't possible, either. Reed had to pop into the lab to print out her work and, just to add insult to injury, bring Noelle along with her. It was as if the girl had known Ariana would be hiding there and had figured out exactly how to hurt her.

Behind her, a pair of girls laughed and Ariana turned toward them. It was Tahira's roommate, Allison Rothaus, and her friend Zuri. They were huddled over a cell phone, scrolling through pictures. The two of them were, of course, strictly second-tier around here. Zuri was in one of the other societies and Allison had failed to make the cut at Stone and Grave. But still. The sight of them together, having fun, made Ariana's spirits drop even lower. They may have been losers, but at least they had each other.

Ariana turned around in her seat again and looked at the empty chairs surrounding the table, feeling suddenly and hopelessly alone. A few weeks ago, Brigit would have been sitting right next to her, gabbing about the next big party. Soomie would have been texting on her BlackBerry obsessively. Lexa would have been perched across the table, flipping through *Vogue* and pointing out who would look best in which outfits. Maria would have been to her left, chugging her espresso and studiously avoiding carbs. But now, Brigit and Lexa were both dead, Soomie was AWOL, and Maria was taking out her grief in the dance studio. Ariana may have been the new It Girl on campus, but that position was supposed to come with an entourage. Hers was practically nonexistent.

"We need to talk."

Tahira dropped into the chair across from Ariana's and just like that, Ariana completely perked up. At least she wasn't sitting in the café looking like a loner anymore.

"What's up?" Ariana asked. "Do you want something to eat? Because I can get Quinn back here in two shakes," she said, reaching for her phone.

"No, thanks." Tahira rested her elbows on the table, her dozens of glittery bangle bracelets clinking merrily. She wore a royal blue, V-neck and her dark hair hung in loose waves over her shoulders. "There's just something I have to ask you. It's kind of serious."

Ariana's heart skipped a troubled beat. Was this about Palmer? Had he finally gotten around to spreading rumors about her?

"You have my undivided attention," Ariana said, trying to sound upbeat.

"Okay, ever since you got here, all this weird stuff has been happening," Tahira began. "I'm not even going to get into the thefts," she said, causing Ariana's stomach to turn. "We're well past that."

Ariana cleared her throat. She'd forgotten about the thefts. Only Tahira knew about them, but that, coupled with anything Palmer might have said, was not going to help her case. She sat up straight as Jessica returned with her sweater.

"Here you go, Ana. Is there anything else I can—"

"No, thank you, Jessica. Just go," Ariana snapped.

Jessica's face crumpled and she hurried off. Ariana clucked her tongue, but the last thing she felt able to deal with at that moment was stroking the ego of an underling. Why was Tahira even mentioning the petty crime Ariana committed at the beginning of term?

"But first Palmer breaks up with Lexa out of nowhere to get with you, and last year those two were totally most likely to hire Colin Cowie," Tahira continued under her breath. "Then Brigit dies, Lillian vanishes, and now Lexa . . ."

Ariana's heart pounded sickly in her throat. She clutched the cashmere sweater under the table, her mind whirling in ten thousand directions. Tahira had figured her out. She knew that it was all connected, and connected through her. The question was, how *much* did she know? Had she found out Ariana's true identity? Was that what had kept her up all night? And what would Ariana have to do to keep her quiet?

"I just need to know," Tahira said, leaning so far forward Ariana could see every inch of her cleavage. "How do you do it all?"

Ariana licked her dry lips. "Do what all?"

"Somehow, with all of this stuff going on around you, you managed to keep your head on straight and come out the other side the queen bee!" Tahira exclaimed, sitting up, her brown eyes wide. "I mean, aside from that slight panic attack the other night, but everyone's had one or two of *those* in their lives. So tell me. How do you do it?"

Ariana let out a *whoosh* of breath. Her tension deflated so quickly she actually slumped forward for a moment, resting her elbows on the table and her head in her hands, her sweater draped across her knees. Tahira wasn't accusing her of masterminding the deaths and disappearances and breakups. She wasn't going to tell her she thought she was crazy, too. She was telling her she thought she was awesome.

"Take your time," Tahira said. She reached for Ariana's scone and tore off a piece. "Omigod! Is that an invite to the MTV New Year's thing?" She snagged the glittery envelope from the top of the pile. Then her eyes widened at the large stack of invitations beneath it. "Wow. It must be good to be president."

Ariana preened. "I suppose so," she said modestly.

"Unbelievable," Tahira said in awe, running her fingers along the edge of the invitation. "Seriously, Ana. You should give, like, a seminar on success or something. Right now, every girl at this school wants to be you."

Now Ariana couldn't help grinning. Tahira had no idea, but this little visit was exactly what she'd needed. Still, there was that niggling problem of Palmer's threat hanging out there like a guillotine ready to drop. Ariana narrowed her eyes and decided that she could trust Tahira, especially after the serious ego-stroking the girl had just given her.

"T, can I ask you something?" she said, resting her elbows casually on the table.

"Anything."

"Has Palmer said anything about me? To you or Rob or anyone?" Ariana asked.

Tahira laughed lightly. "Oh, you mean that ridiculous story about you trashing your room? Uh, yeah. I heard that one."

"You did?" Ariana asked, her face flushed.

Tahira grabbed another piece of scone. "Like anyone's gonna believe that. You're the second most anal person I know, after Soomie," Tahira said as she chewed. "And honestly, even if you *did* trash your room, who cares? Everyone's gotta vent somehow, especially with everything that's been going on. The other day me and Rob went to his dad's shooting range and went ballistic on the targets with actual shotguns. It was *so* therapeutic."

Ariana blinked. "Um. Wow."

"Yeah. No one's gonna be judging you for breaking your own stuff. Believe me," Tahira said firmly. "And all Palmer did by bringing it up out of nowhere was make himself look like a sore loser and, honestly? Kind of a dick."

Ariana laughed under her breath. Talk about a plan backfiring. Too bad for Palmer. "That's good to know. Thanks, Tahira."

"I just can't believe you have to run S and G with him as your second-in-command. That's not gonna be awkward or anything," Tahira said sarcastically, rolling her eyes.

Ariana curled her hands around her coffee cup. With everything else that was going on, she hadn't even thought of that. Palmer was still the vice president of Stone and Grave. And he clearly hated her. His first play for power seemed to be unsuccessful, but that didn't mean he wouldn't keep trying. Perhaps it was time to start thinking of ways to get rid of him. Maybe it would be a good thing if he kept talking crap about her around campus. If *everyone* started to think he was a sore loser and a dick, it would be far easier to gather support for his removal.

Tahira's phone beeped and she tugged it out of her bag. "Crap. I was supposed to meet Rob and his parents at the gates ten minutes ago," she said as she stood up again. "They're flying back to Florida today and we said we'd have breakfast with them. Yee. Ha."

Ariana laughed.

"Hey, do you want to do some shopping tomorrow?" Tahira asked, lowering her voice. "I personally believe that the president of Stone and Grave should have a signature look to be envied by all. And I'm not talking about that sunglasses-at-night look."

"Absolutely," Ariana replied. "We can make a plan later."

"Perfect," Tahira said. She leaned down and double-air-kissed Ariana. "Then maybe I can pick your brain about how you do it all."

She winked before whirling away and disappearing through the Privilege House doors. Ariana watched her go, her confidence entirely recovered. Apparently Palmer didn't wield quite as much power as he thought. And Tahira was right, after all. Look at all she'd been through in her life, and she always, *always* found a way to land on her feet. Yesterday's blip with Reed had been just that—a blip. All she needed to do was rethink, retrench, come up with a new, foolproof plan. Before long, Reed Brennan would be dead, and Ariana would be one step closer to the perfect life she'd always wanted.

HOLDING OUT

"Okay, I need one of these in every color."

Tahira grabbed a fringed leather Jimmy Choo bag and slung it over her shoulder, posing in front of the full-length mirror. Ariana had already done some serious damage to her credit cards, buying a whole new wardrobe for her position of power. She'd purchased so much, in fact, that she'd left all her packages with the store's valet to have them shipped back to school, knowing they wouldn't fit in the trunk of her tiny car.

"It *is* very you," Ariana replied as she considered a mustard-colored Michael Kors clutch.

"What do you think, Maria?" Tahira asked, whipping around dramatically. "Isn't it just yum?"

Maria glanced over from her perch atop a Lucite table filled with sale merchandise. "Eh," she said.

Tahira's shoulders dropped and the bag slid to her wrist. "Eh? You've got to be kidding me."

"Sorry. Fringe isn't really my thing," Maria said, lifting her slim shoulders.

"Well, I love it," Tahira replied. She walked over to the counter and plopped the black bag down in front of the saleslady. "I'll take the red, the white, and the green as well."

The saleswoman's dark eyes widened, probably seeing her monthly commission triple in one fell swoop. Tahira had just committed herself to about five thousand dollars' worth of purses.

"Are you getting that?" Tahira asked Ariana.

Ariana replaced the bag on its shelf. "I think I've spent enough for one night," she said, even though she could have bought a million clutch bags with the green she had in her bank account, thanks to Grandma Covington's recent death.

"Well, maybe your new *boyfriend* will get it for you for Christmas," Tahira said, her voice leading. She slapped her credit card down on the counter as the saleswoman returned from the display with her other bags.

Ariana smirked. She'd wondered when this subject would come up. Now that the wound of Lexa's death wasn't quite so fresh and the Stone and Grave presidency had been decided, of course Jasper would be the next bit of gossip to occupy everyone's minds.

"Yeah, what's up with that anyway?" Maria asked, leaning her palms into the display table across from Ariana. "One second you're dumping Palmer, all heartbroken, and the next second you're canoodling with the Louisiana blondie."

Ariana lifted a shoulder. "It just kind of . . . happened."

"Oh, please. You're not getting off that easily," Tahira said, watching with one eye as the saleslady placed her purchases into their cushy boxes. "I mean, Jasper's a cutie, don't get me wrong. But Palmer is . . . Palmer."

"And Palmer's a jerk," Maria put in.

"Yes, but only *since* the breakup," Tahira reminded them.

"I don't know. Jasper and I bonded during pledging and there was always something intriguing about him," Ariana said with a blush. She dragged her finger across a row of hanging Coach keychains, letting them swing and clink together. "Palmer was always very by-the-book, very black-and-white and predictable. But Jasper is . . . surprising."

Maria grinned and raised her eyebrows. "Sounds delish."

Ariana's blush deepened. "You have no idea."

"Okay. Now *I'm* intrigued," Tahira said, tossing her dark hair over her shoulder. "And starved. I say you spill all the *delish* details over tapas."

"I could be in for that," Maria said.

"Me too. But you have to eat more than one thing," Ariana said, raising a warning finger at Maria.

"Who said you get to mother me?" Maria said good-naturedly. "You're the one we've got to keep an eye on around here, Miss Panic Attack."

Ariana's skin prickled. If she could take back anything from the past few days it would be having that minor breakdown in front of her friends. She didn't want them to worry about her. But even more importantly, she didn't want them to lose confidence in her, especially with Palmer talking crap about her behind her back. Maybe Tahira hadn't cared, but that didn't mean everyone would be so open-minded. She needed to project a self-assured, in-charge, *sane* image, not that of a weakling who could crumble at any second.

"That was a fluke," she told Maria, looping her arm around her friend's. "It won't happen again, I promise. I'm fine."

"Ready?" Tahira asked, joining them with two massive bags dangling from either hand.

"Ready."

As the girls walked out of the department store and onto the dark, frigid street, Ariana fished her car keys from her bag. She hit the UNLOCK button and the headlights on her sleek, silver sports car flashed. With another click, she popped the trunk for Tahira's bags. She and Maria waited on the sidewalk while Tahira loaded her things inside and slammed the door.

"So, Ana, how long did you think you were going to be able to hold out on us?" she asked, leaning one red-gloved hand against the trunk.

Ariana blinked. "Hold out on you? About what? Jasper?"

"No." Tahira brushed her leather gloves off as she rejoined them on the sidewalk. "I was on the APH student site today and they had a list of all the upcoming birthdays. Someone we know was on it!" she said, singing the last few words.

Ariana's brow knit, and then suddenly her heart thumped extra hard against her rib cage. Briana Leigh's birthday! It was December 12. How could she have possibly forgotten?

"Ana! It's your birthday?" Maria asked, her eyes widening with delight. "When?"

Ariana finally forced herself to blush and looked down at her feet.

"Next week. I guess I don't really feel much like celebrating," she improvised, drawing an arc on the silty concrete with the toe of her suede boot. "Besides, wouldn't it be a little selfish right now? Making myself the center of attention?"

"Gimme a break," Tahira said, rolling her eyes as she headed for the passenger side door. "I am *totally* throwing you a party."

Ariana's heart fluttered in excitement. She hadn't been able to celebrate her election as Stone and Grave president, but this would more than make up for that.

"You don't have to do that," she said.

"Just try to stop me," Tahira said, narrowing her eyes.

"Yeah, I wouldn't try to stop her," Maria joked. "You know what? Maybe I'll help. It'll give me something to distract me from Lexa and the Soomie situation."

"Cool. Just as long as we're clear that all final decisions are mine," Tahira said.

Maria smirked. "Ma'am, yes, ma'am."

Ariana gave them a small, modest smile. "Okay. Thanks, guys. Just . . . don't go overboard."

Tahira shot Maria a look that clearly said "Yeah, right." As they all piled into Ariana's car, Ariana bit down on her lip to keep from giggling out loud. She had a feeling Tahira was going to throw the party to end all parties, all for her.

Ariana dropped into the bucket seat behind the wheel and her phone let out a loud beep. She fished it from the bottom of her bag.

"Hang on a sec. I have a voice mail," she said.

"Make it quick. I'm starting to feel faint," Tahira said, flipping the visor down to check her eye makeup in the mirror.

Ariana dialed into voice mail and held the phone to her ear. The voice that greeted her stopped her blood cold.

"Hello, Miss Covington, this is Dr. Victor Meloni, calling to inform you that your mandatory session has been scheduled for tomorrow, Monday the eighth, at ten a.m. in my office on the third floor of the administration building. Looking forward to seeing you then. Have a good night."

The message ended with a loud beep, and Ariana flinched, but found she otherwise couldn't move. She sat there for a long moment, staring at the streetlights outside the windshield, the phone stuck to her ear.

"Ana? Ana, hello? Are you in there?" Tahira asked, waving a mascara wand in front of her face.

"You look sickly again. Was that bad news? Was it Soomie?" Maria asked, leaning in from the miniscule backseat.

"No. No, it was nothing. Sorry. I just spaced for a second there," Ariana said. She pushed down on the DELETE button so hard she was surprised the phone didn't shatter, then tossed the phone in the well between her seat and Tahira's. "So. Tapas?"

She revved the engine, threw the car into gear, and lurched out onto the street. Her fingers gripped the wheel as her jaw clenched so tightly she felt a pain in her temple. Hearing Meloni's insipid voice on the phone, the authoritative tone he took while demanding her presence in his office, had brought home the urgency of the situation. She could not allow him within six feet of her or all would be lost. But she couldn't avoid him, either. As he'd so helpfully mentioned, all student sessions with the grief counselor were mandatory.

As Ariana took a corner at top speed, eliciting a squeak of fear from Tahira's throat, she knew with a cold certainty that the plan was going to have to change. She had wanted to do away with Reed first and then deal with Meloni, but obviously Reed's death was going to be put on the backburner for now.

As of this moment, her number-one priority was ridding the world of Dr. Victor Meloni.

TOO EASY

Late Monday afternoon, Ariana begged out of her lit magazine meeting early, telling April she was late for a chemistry study group. She had, in fact, moved her car to the faculty lot behind the Administration Building that afternoon and planned to wait in it until Dr. Meloni left work for the night. She needed to follow him, needed to find out where he was living, needed to start formulating her plan. Once Meloni was gone, she could get back to Reed. And she was very much looking forward to getting back to Reed.

Quickly, she scurried across the frost-covered campus, hoping against hope that Dr. Meloni had yet to leave for the night. She finally got into her car just as the sun was disappearing behind the trees, and started the engine, relishing in the warmth from the heaters and keeping an eye on the back door of the Administration Building. Luckily, she wasn't too late. Within minutes, Dr. Meloni emerged. Blowing into his hands, he unhooked Rambo from his running line and opened the passenger side door of a gold Lincoln Tahoe for the dog. Moments later, he was behind the wheel, and they were off.

"Let's see what kind of place you've bought for yourself on my tuition's dime," Ariana muttered under her breath as she followed from a discreet distance.

She had skipped their mandatory meeting that morning without so much as a phone call to make an excuse and had kept her phone off all day, dreading his reaction. Now she wondered if he'd called her yet, or if he was going to leave it to the headmaster to deal with her scolding and punishment.

Ariana laughed bitterly to herself. No. No way. Meloni would certainly make sure he got to do all the scolding and belittling on his own. It was probably written into his contract.

Meloni headed away from the city and into the hills on the Virginia side of the capital. The move didn't surprise Ariana in the slightest. Back at the Brenda T., Dr. Meloni had resided in a small cabin set back on a dirt road. She was certain he made a ton of money and could have lived anywhere he wished, but instead he'd chosen a spartan existence, living like a colonial mountain man. No doubt he did it to make some kind of point—that he was a man's man, or above the trappings of modern society, or some crap like that.

Ariana squinted against the dark as Meloni turned onto a slim, two-lane road, lined with towering, bare trees. When he suddenly pulled off into a circular driveway, Ariana's heart hit her throat. She couldn't exactly turn in after him. Thinking fast, she kept right on driving, but she cursed under her breath, realizing she hadn't gotten a good look at the house.

"Okay, it's okay," she told herself, adjusting her sweaty palms on the wheel. "Just turn around and go back."

She pulled into a small clearing at the side of the road, counted slowly to one hundred, then flipped a U-turn and drove back to Meloni's. She made sure to drive at a snail's pace so that she could take it all in. The Tahoe was dark in the driveway—the only car parked there. A light glowed in one of the front windows of a long, low ranch house. It was bigger than the place he'd called home back at the Brenda T., but still unassuming. Ariana killed the Porsche's lights and pulled off the side of the road. There didn't appear to be a security system, and the closest streetlight was half a mile away. She sat for a long time, staring at that light in the window, but seeing no movement. An hour passed, then another. And in all that time, Ariana saw but one car go by.

Finally, the light went out, and a moment later another went on upstairs. Clearly, Meloni still lived alone. And on a street that hardly a soul ever passed through. Satisfied, Ariana slowly rolled out onto the road and drove a few yards before turning on her headlights again. Then she opened up the engine and floored it, headed back toward town with a huge, happy grin.

Good old Dr. Meloni. He really couldn't have made this much easier on her.

MENTAL HEALTH

Thanks to her jaunt through the Virginia woodlands, Ariana was so late to dinner on Monday evening, her friends were already packing up to leave when she arrived.

"We were just on our way over to the Hill," Maria said, slinging her scarf over her forearm and her messenger bag onto her shoulder. Behind her, Tahira shoved her cell phone and some books into her bag. "Want us to wait? We can sit with you if you want."

"No, that's okay," Ariana replied. After the excitement of her recon mission, she relished the idea of sitting quietly and organizing her thoughts. "I'll meet you there when I'm done."

"Cool. We'll save you a seat," Tahira said.

The girls walked off together to the junior/senior lounge, which was through a set of heavy double doors at the far end of the dining hall. Ariana sat down, placing her last-minute order with the waiter. She saw several people eye her curiously as they left, including Palmer and his little pack of followers, but she ignored them. Couldn't a girl be late for dinner anymore without becoming the subject of gossip?

Once her meal arrived, Ariana ate it slowly, meticulously reviewing the route she'd taken to Meloni's house over and over again so that she wouldn't forget a thing. She was definitely going to have to go back there again soon, at a time when he wasn't home, to survey the perimeter, see if there were any good points of entry, and make absolutely sure he didn't have a girlfriend—gag—or someone who might show up unexpectedly. Once she'd decided on this course of action, she pulled up her schedule on her phone. This was something she was going to need to accomplish quickly, before another "mandatory" meeting was set up for her. As she eyed her class schedule, she realized that she was going to have to skip class no matter what. The middle of the workday was the only time she could ensure Meloni wouldn't be around. But she'd already missed so much thanks to Reed, and finals were coming up. . . . Ariana let out a frustrated sigh. She really was juggling a lot these days.

Finally, she decided to just skip out on Spanish the next day and get it over with. She was carrying an A average in that course as it was. Missing one more class couldn't do much harm. Satisfied, Ariana slipped her phone back into her bag, finished her meal, and thanked the waiter. Then she gathered her coat, scarf, hat, and bag up in her arms and headed across the room to join her friends at the Hill.

She had just walked through the door when Headmaster Jansen stepped up next to her. It was as if the woman had been lying in wait.

"Miss Covington?"

CRUEL LOVE 151

Ariana closed her eyes for a moment, steeling herself, then turned with a big smile.

"Hi, Headmaster. How are you?" she asked.

"I'm fine, thank you. I'm more interested in how you're doing." She reached out and grasped Ariana's forearm quickly, her expression the picture of concern. "I heard you missed a few days of classes and skipped your mandatory meeting with your grief counselor this morning."

"Yes, I was planning to reschedule that."

"Were you?" the headmaster said sternly.

Ariana felt her skin redden. How dare this woman doubt her? What had she ever done to earn that?

"Of course," she replied. "It was just a rough week for me. I did lose my best friend in the most horrific way possible."

"All the more reason to see the counselor," the headmaster said.

A few senior girls hovered behind Ariana, angling to get through the door. She clucked her tongue and stepped away from the entrance, letting them through. She knew there was a way to spin this. She just had to think of it. Now. She tucked her new and insanely expensive angora scarf into her bag, and just like that, it hit her.

Money. It all came back to money. And Ariana, thanks to the recent death of Briana Leigh's grandmother, had tons of it at her disposal.

"Headmaster, to be honest . . . I was hoping to hire my own counselor, if that would be at all possible," Ariana said. "I'd be more than willing to have him or her sign some sort of document confirming I'd completed a session."

The headmaster's perfectly groomed brows creased. She crossed her slim arms over her stylishly cut suit. "Why?"

Ariana bit her lip. "It's just . . . I've heard some not-so-pleasant things about this Doctor Meloni," she lied, bile burning the back of her throat as she uttered the name. "My friends who have seen him . . . they don't get anything out of their sessions. And one of them mentioned feeling condescended to. Now, I don't know about you, but that doesn't sound like the role of a grief counselor to me."

"That's odd. I've had only positive feedback from the students on Dr. Meloni," the headmaster said.

Ariana gritted her teeth. "Well, maybe they just haven't wanted to upset you."

The headmaster's eyes narrowed. "I see. The problem is, Miss Covington, that Doctor Meloni is very interested in meeting you."

The entire room tilted so suddenly before Ariana's eyes, she was forced to reach out and grab the back of the nearest sofa. She brought her fingertips to her forehead for a moment and closed her eyes. "I'm sorry. What? Why?"

"He said he knows something of your family history," the headmaster replied. "To be quite honest, from the way he spoke about you, I got the impression the two of you already knew each other."

"What?" Ariana's eyes popped open, but her vision had already prickled over. She could barely make out the headmaster's face.

"Have you ever been a patient of his before?" the headmaster asked.

"No! No, of course not," Ariana replied, shaking her head, trying to clear her eyes, her mind. Had Dr. Meloni seen her that night on campus with Maria and Tahira? Did he know she was here? Was he just licking his chops, waiting for her to walk into his office like some kind of injured lamb?

But no. It wasn't possible. He'd looked up for half a second that night and it had been pitch-black out. All he would have seen were Ariana's black hat, her auburn hair, her dark sunglasses. He never would have recognized her under those conditions.

"There's no shame in it, Briana Leigh," the headmaster said. "Everyone needs someone to talk to at some point in their lives."

"I'm telling you I *don't* know him," Ariana said, her voice strained.

"All I know is that when he saw the name Briana Leigh Covington on the list of students, he said he thought he'd be uniquely suited to help you," Headmaster Jansen said, raising a palm.

Suddenly, Ariana felt a cool *whoosh* of air down her back. Briana Leigh Covington. Of course. Dr. Meloni had treated Kaitlynn Nottingham inside the Brenda T., and Kaitlynn had been arrested for murdering Briana Leigh's father in cold blood. Dr. Meloni knew something about *Briana Leigh's* family history because of his association with Kaitlynn. He had no idea Ariana was masquerading as the girl whose name he'd recognized.

Taking in a deep, cleansing breath, Ariana pulled herself up straight and focused on the headmaster's eyes.

"I've never heard of this person in my life, yet he claims some prior connection and interest in me? That didn't raise any red flags for you?" Ariana said.

The headmaster blinked, clearly taken aback. "I didn't think—"

"And if it's so important to you that I see someone—if it's so important to my mental health—shouldn't you allow me to see someone with whom I feel comfortable, rather than some random man who might turn out to be a stalker?" Ariana asked through her teeth.

"I hardly think—"

"When I enrolled at this school, my grandmother made a very generous donation to the general education fund, a donation which I intended to duplicate upon my graduation," Ariana continued, "but if I start to feel that my needs aren't being met here, I might have to rethink the whole thing."

Suddenly the headmaster's jaw set. She wiped her palms on the skirt of her suit and cleared her throat. It was clear from the irritation in her eyes that she knew she was being played and didn't like it.

"Of course, I would never want any of my students to feel as if their needs weren't being met," she said, her words clipped. "If you feel you'd rather see someone off campus, we'll see what we can do."

Slowly, Ariana smiled. *I really do have all the power,* she thought giddily. "Thank you," Ariana said curtly. "Now if you'll excuse me."

"Of course."

Ariana stepped around the headmaster, a triumphant grin nearly splitting her face. Suddenly the Meloni situation didn't feel quite so urgent. She wasn't going to have to meet with him, which meant she had just scored herself more time to make sure she came up with the perfect plan for his execution. All she had to do was make sure she avoided him on campus and she would be fine. Could this day get any better?

She spotted Maria and Tahira at a prime table near one of the bay windows and waved, but hesitated. There was someone missing from this picture, and suddenly she felt more empowered than ever to do something about it. She held up a finger to her friends, telling them she'd be there in a second, then found an empty chair and took out her phone.

"Please just answer. Just this once," she said under her breath. Then she speed-dialed Soomie's cell phone.

This time, the connection did not go straight to voice mail. In fact, it rang three times and suddenly, Ariana heard the sound of fumbling, then breathing, then a voice.

"Ana. Hey."

Soomie sounded tired and distant. Like she was talking to her from another galaxy.

"Hi! Oh my God, Soomie! It's so good to hear your voice!" Ariana said breathlessly. She clutched the phone tightly to her ear, as if doing so could somehow prevent Soomie from disconnecting.

"Yeah, I'm . . . I got all your messages. I'm sorry I haven't called back," Soomie said.

"That's okay. Where are you? Are you all right?" Ariana asked, curling her legs up beneath her on the chair cushion.

"I'm . . . fine. Better, I guess. I'm in Antigua with my mom. We've been staying at this spa where they don't allow TV or phones or Internet," Soomie replied. "I'm hiding in a closet right now, actually."

Ariana got a mental picture of Soomie curled into a ball on the floor of a small, dark room, wooden hangers dangling above her.

"That's intense," she said. "How much longer are you guys going to be there?"

"I don't know," Soomie said. "It's an open-ended stay. My mom's on top of me all the time. She's, like, afraid I'm gonna snap or something. I keep telling her the only thing that's going to make me snap is having her fawn all over me, but it's like talking to a wall."

Ariana laughed, and she heard Soomie exhale a chuckle, too. That had to be a good sign.

"But it *is* kind of nice, to be honest," Soomie said. "Not knowing what's going on in the real world. There's no stress, no worry. I've been sleeping. A lot."

Because there's probably some "spa doctor" feeding you muscle relaxers, Ariana thought, biting her lip.

"That doesn't sound like you," Ariana said carefully. "You're the busiest person I know, usually."

"I know," Soomie said, somewhere between sad and wistful.

"It sounds like you miss it," Ariana said, holding her breath.

"I did. I mean, I do." Ariana heard jostling in the background, and imagined Soomie pushing herself up off the floor. "I miss the distraction, I guess. Whenever I'm not sleeping, I'm thinking. Wondering if there was something I missed. Something I could have done."

"I've spent a lot of time doing that, too," Ariana replied. A pair of senior boys dropped down onto the couch adjacent to her chair, and she turned slightly away from them. When she did, she found herself looking right at Palmer, who sat in the far corner, drinking bottled iced tea with some of his friends. Suddenly, an idea occurred to her. A brilliant idea that could benefit both herself and Soomie. "But, Soomie, it's pointless. There's no going back. You know what's really helped me?"

"What?" Soomie asked.

"Focusing on my future," Ariana said. She fiddled with the clasp on her bag, opening it and closing it over and over again, excitement ticking her veins. "I've been getting some college brochures together and narrowing down my choices . . . and I don't know if you've heard, but I was elected president of Stone and Grave."

"You were?" Soomie suddenly came to life. "Ana! Congratulations!"

"Thank you," Ariana replied, blushing. "And, well, Palmer's been pretty out of it so I think we may need to elect a new V. P.," she continued slowly. "I think you'd be perfect for the job."

"Wow. I . . . that could be cool," Soomie said.

"You could have as much or as little responsibility as you want," Ariana put in, warming to her subject. She watched Palmer yuck it up with his buddies as she talked, imagining how stunned he'd be when she asked him to step down and suggested Soomie as his replacement. "I bet if you got back here and got involved . . . if you threw yourself back into your school work . . . I know you'd feel so much better."

There was a long pause. Ariana could hear Soomie's breathing, and imagined she could hear her considering, too.

"Besides, we miss you, Soomie," Ariana said, lowering her voice a bit, tempering her tone. "Maria misses you. . . . I really feel we'll all get through this so much better if we do it together."

"Ana, I—"

Ariana heard Soomie's voice catch and thought she was about to cry. But then, a furtive whisper came through.

"Crap. That's my mom. I've gotta go."

"Wait, Soomie. Promise you'll think about what I said," Ariana whispered back.

"I will. Thanks, Ana. Bye."

And just like that, it was over. Ariana ended the call and sat for a moment, listening to the buzz of conversation around her and feeling highly alert. She hoped Soomie wasn't getting into trouble with her mom. She hoped what she'd said to her friend had gotten through. Because she really wanted Soomie to get her life back. But she also needed to replace her obnoxious ex as soon as humanly possible. And most important, once she figured out how to deal with Meloni, she wanted to have her entourage firmly in place.

BENEVOLENCE

Ariana turned on her phone after her last class of the day on Tuesday and it instantly let out a beep, indicating that she had a new message. She shouldered her bag and turned her steps toward the library, holding the phone to her ear.

"Miss Covington, this is Doctor Victor Meloni."

Ariana almost tripped on an uneven brick in the pathway. She paused to catch her breath and glanced around to make sure no one had noticed her near fall. All around her, students rushed from class in clumps and pairs, headed toward their dorms or their clubs or their practices. Ariana took a deep breath and kept walking, Dr. Meloni yammering on in her ear. She just could not escape from this jerk.

"I've spoken to the headmaster and I'm going to assume from her account of your conversation that you somehow know of my connection to your father's killer, Kaitlynn Nottingham," the message continued. "I believed that my unique insight into your history might enable me to help you in a real way, but clearly you disagree."

Ariana jogged up the stone steps to the library and stopped outside the door, leaning back against the wrought-iron railing. Kassie Sharpe strolled by and gave her a quick wave, so Ariana did her best to shoot her a friendly smile.

She could not believe the know-it-all, condescending tone Dr. Meloni was taking with her voice mail. Wait. Yes she could. This was Dr. Victor Meloni, after all. Did he ever say anything that wasn't know-it-all and condescending?

"Therefore, the headmaster has decided to allow you to seek outside help and I have, against my better judgment, acquiesced. Because, Miss Covington, the most important thing is that you talk to someone and receive some help. Even if that someone might not be the most qualified person for the job. In case you feel the need to speak to someone else after this outside meeting, please know that my door is always open, and I'd be more than happy to speak with you over the phone, if that makes you more comfortable. Have a good day."

The beep sounded, indicating the end of the message. Ariana gritted her teeth and pressed her thumb down on the DELETE button until she thought the phone might crack. What an asshole. What a complete, indisputable asshole. The world was going to be a much better place without a guy like Victor Meloni polluting it with his toxic positing and self-rightousness.

But at least the immediate danger was officially over. She would not be forced to meet with the man who could instantly end her existence. That was a great relief. But he still had to go. He was a loose end, a liability.

With another deep, cleansing breath, Ariana tucked her short auburn hair behind her ear and strode into the library, her head held high. She walked to the back of the study carrels and found an empty desk, where she quickly plugged in her laptop. Her plan for the evening had been to start organizing her notes for her chemistry final, but now she knew there was no way she would be able to concentrate on that sort of menial task. Not until she got some planning out of the way first.

Ariana shed her coat, sat down, and jumped her chair forward until her rib cage was pressed firmly against the edge of the desk. She blew out a breath and pushed her hair back from her face with both hands.

Killing Dr. Meloni was going to be different. The man was older, wiser, and more physically powerful than anyone she'd ever dealt with before. There had been times in the past, times she wasn't exactly proud of, when the killing had come out of nowhere. It had sprung from sudden and violent emotions, like when she'd lost her cool with Thomas Pearson. Or simple convenient twists of fate, like that day she'd let Sergei Tretyakov drown in the lake near the Easton campus. She had planned out Kaitlynn's murder rather meticulously, but that had been necessary. Kaitlynn, like Meloni, was smart and intuitive with serious reflexes, not to mention a killer survival instinct. So Meloni, like Kaitlynn, required a plan.

Ariana opened a new Word document and started to organize her to-do list. She typed it up quickly, glancing over her shoulder every so often to make sure no one was near enough to see her screen.

> *Get his schedule down to the minute*
> *Visit his house again. Check for:*
>   *Security system*
>   *Points of entry*
>   *Evidence of other residents*
>   *Heavy traffic times (probably none)*
>   *Place to park the car least visible from road*
> *Work on handwriting*

Here, Ariana paused and closed her eyes, thinking back to the Brenda T. She had no problem envisioning Dr. Meloni's signature. He'd written it on every chart, every prescription order, every report, every demerit. But most of the documents had been typed up on a computer, then signed by hand. Biting her bottom lip, she opened her eyes again. There was no way she would be able to write out the entire suicide note. Even if she broke into his on-campus office, she was fairly certain she wouldn't be able to find enough writing samples to perfect his handwriting.

"I'll have to type it out, print it, then sign it," she murmured under her breath. "That's what he would do anyway."

She went back to her list of things to do at his house and added:

> *Location of computer?*

Then she recalled another serious necessity and added that as well.

Find his gun
If no gun, must buy one.
   Find out what one needs to buy a gun legally
   Consider illegal avenues???
Buy treats/meat for Rambo distraction

Ariana sat back in her chair and blew out a breath. She was feeling much calmer, more peaceful, than she had while listening to Meloni's message. This was going to be fine. It was going to be perfect, actually. The only question was when? When would Dr. Victor Meloni meet his end?

Smiling, Ariana imagined how the whole thing would play out. Imagined the look of shock on his face when he recognized her. How sweet it would all be. She could hardly wait.

"But you have to," she whispered to herself. "Reed comes first, then Meloni. You've bought yourself time. Just remember that. You have time."

Ariana clicked open her calendar and scanned it. The next few weeks were going to be so busy, with studying for finals, her big birthday bash, Stone and Grave events, and getting ready for Christmas break. She narrowed her eyes as she scanned the dates, and finally decided everything could wait at least until after her birthday party that Friday night. She deserved to have a little stress-free fun. Once all the champagne had been popped, all the cake devoured, and all the presents opened, then she could deal with the tasks at hand.

Both Reed Brennan and Dr. Meloni had just been granted a slight reprieve, and they didn't even know it. Ariana smiled, saved her document and opened her chem notes, feeling like a benevolent saint—putting her own needs aside and granting her victims a few more precious days of life.

RESIGNATION

As Ariana led her fellow Stone and Grave members into the cave for her first official meeting as president, she tried as hard as she could to force a solemn expression onto her face. She fixed her eyes on the candle closest to the place of honor she would now occupy and stared it down, attempting to think somber thoughts. Thoughts about death and responsibility and privilege. But she just couldn't do it. The giddy bubbles that had danced inside of her chest all afternoon had pumped up the party to a frenzied roar, and try as she might, there was just no keeping the ridiculous grin off her face.

She was president of Stone and Grave. She was *president* of *Stone and Grave*!

Now that she had started to plan for Meloni's demise, she had resolved not to think about Dr. Meloni or Reed Brennan anymore. At least not for today. She wanted to enjoy this moment. She wanted to relish it. She was not going to let old enemies ruin one of the biggest accomplishments of her new life. As she slowly made the circuit of the room, she took a deep breath and let any negative inklings melt swiftly away.

This was her night and hers alone. No one could taint it. And just to put the capper on the occasion, Soomie had shown up at the last minute and joined the processional. It looked as if things were really starting to return to the way they should be.

At the top of the circle, Ariana paused and faced inward. Palmer should have been directly to her left, but once again he'd decided not to show—unknowingly giving her great ammunition for her remove-Palmer-as-V. P. plan. Instead, Soomie was next in line. After her came April, Conrad, Maria, and so on down the line, until Jasper finally brought up the very rear. Ariana glanced at Tahira and Landon, at the spot between them that she used to occupy—a spot for lowly neophytes—and it was all she could do to keep from giggling out loud.

Christian Thacker stepped from the circle to close the heavy doors silently. When he returned to his place, Ariana took a moment to relish her position, before speaking.

"We are the Stone and Grave!"

"We are the Stone and Grave!" the membership replied.

Ariana smiled. "You may all be seated."

Candles flickered and robes swooshed as the membership settled themselves in on the ground. Ariana smiled at Soomie and turned to face the group.

"Before I open the floor to new business, I just wanted to say thank you all for granting me the honor of the presidency," Ariana began, rolling her shoulders back. "I appreciate your confidence in me, and I want you to know that I won't let you down."

"Here, here!" Adam shouted, inspiring a round of applause.

Ariana smiled bashfully and raised a hand to silence them. "I'd also like to welcome Sister Emma Woodhouse back from her vacation," Ariana added. "We missed you, Sister. Everyone's so glad to see you here and healthy."

Another round of applause. Soomie blushed and looked down at her lap. "I wouldn't be here if it weren't for you, Sister Portia, and you, Sister Estella," Soomie said to Ariana and Maria when the noise died down. She looked up and addressed the room. "Over the past couple of weeks, Sisters Portia and Estella have shown me what true friendship and dedication really mean. While I would have preferred to have been here for something as important as an emergency election, I'm glad you all saw the same things in Sister Portia that I've seen. And I'm glad to be back," she added, her eyes shining.

"We're glad to have you!" Maria said, reaching in for a hug.

"Awwww. It's like a bad episode of *The View*," Rob joked, earning a round of laughter from the guys.

"Are there good episodes of *The View*?" Jasper inquired.

"All right, all right. We'll dispense with the sentiment," Ariana said. "Does anyone have any new business?"

"I do, Sister Portia," Christian said, raising a hand. He pushed himself up from the floor and crossed the circle to hand her a note, written on heavy ivory parchment paper. Ariana recognized Palmer's handwriting instantly, and her heart lurched.

"What's this?" Ariana asked.

Christian shrugged. "Brother Starbuck asked me to give it to you at the start of the meeting."

He quickly returned to his spot. The paper trembled slightly in Ariana's grip as every single pair of eyes in the room was trained on her. What was Palmer doing? Having his friend pass her notes in the middle of her first official meeting? Was this another attempt at undermining her authority? Making her look silly?

"I think he wanted you to read it out loud," Christian said.

Ariana shot him a look. Like that was going to happen. "I think I'll read it to myself, first."

Carefully she unfolded the note. It was short—only five lines— and what she read made her jaw drop.

"What is it?" Soomie asked.

Ariana rolled her eyes and cleared her throat. "To the Brotherhood of the Stone and Grave," she read aloud. "Due to recent events I find I am unable to, in good conscience, continue my membership in this once-prestigious chapter of this hallowed society. Please accept my sincere regrets, but I must hereby render my resignation. Sincerely, Palmer Liriano."

Suddenly the room erupted in whispers and chatter.

"Who *resigns* from Stone and Grave?"

"He's gotta be kidding."

"Doesn't he realize he just made enemies of all the alumni?"

Ariana folded the letter, reinforcing the fold with a violent slip of her fingers, then shoved it toward April.

"I believe you're going to need that for our records."

April took the note and tossed it into her notebook, slamming the cover over it. Ariana felt her blood pressure slowly rising, her heartbeat thrumming angrily in her ears. Palmer had done this to punish her. Clearly he was trying to show the brotherhood that he thought her so unworthy he'd sacrifice everything Stone and Grave offered just to oppose her.

Well, it was his loss. And in truth, he'd done her a huge favor. Palmer was out. She would never have to deal with him again.

"Silence, please!" Ariana shouted.

It took a couple of moments, but after some shushing from other members, the cave finally fell quiet. Ariana took in a long, deep breath and blew it out through her nose. She would *not* let the brotherhood see her sweat. Palmer had no idea what he was talking about. Ariana *did* deserve to be here. She was a straight-A student, a valued member of the tennis team and the lit magazine, she'd stood out in her pledge class, and Soomie had basically credited her and Maria for bringing her back from the edge. No one at this school deserved to be president of Stone and Grave more than she did.

"Well," Ariana said finally, calmly. "It looks as if we're going to need a new vice president."

She glanced at Soomie and grinned, looking for all the world like Palmer's note, his opinion, couldn't have mattered less.

"Are there any nominations?"

BACK ON TRACK

"Welcome back, Soomie!"

Maria lifted her glass of sparkling water in a toast as Ariana and Tahira cheered. Soomie blushed and clinked glasses with them over the table in the center of one of Soomie's favorite DC locales, Busboys and Poets. It was a cozy, dimly lit grill and bar on one side, and a well-stocked independent bookstore on the other—a place Soomie frequented so often she knew the waitstaff by name.

"We would have come up with something far more fabulous if you'd given us a little notice," Tahira lamented, sipping her soda. She'd been thwarted when she'd tried to order a red wine and the waiter had laughed at her fake ID. The girl had been pouting ever since.

"Actually, this is great," Soomie said, placing her glass down. "It's perfect." She took a deep breath and blew it out. "It's good to be back."

"It's good to have you back," Ariana said with a warm smile.

"Thanks." Soomie sat up a bit straighter as their salads arrived. A raucous group of tweed-clad men by the bar laughed loudly, and the decibel level in the room seemed to grow. "And besides, it sounds like these two are throwing you the party of the decade tomorrow, so that should be plenty fabulous for me," Soomie said, raising her voice to be heard over the din.

"Party of the decade, huh?" Ariana asked, eyeing Maria and Tahira with interest. "Sounds like you guys have been hard at work."

"You have no idea," Maria said with a sigh. She plucked an olive slice off her salad, popped it in her mouth and pointed across the small square table at Tahira. "This one's a slave driver."

"All for a good cause," Tahira replied blithely. "Does the president of S and G deserve anything less?"

Ariana grinned. She loved how everyone kept bringing up her new position of power. Now that she'd run her first meeting, even more calls and gifts had been rolling in, all from Stone and Grave members in high places. After opening up the truckload of boxes the UPS driver had delivered right to her door that morning, she was now the proud owner of a full set of Tocca candles, two iPads, a new laptop, a mink coat, the entire Ralph Lauren spring line, and more baubles and jewels than she could count.

As her friends dug into their salads, Ariana's phone began to vibrate next to her plate. She shot the girls an apologetic look and eyed the screen. After all, a woman in her position couldn't just ignore calls, texts, and e-mails. What if it was important S and G business? The

e-mail was from a name she vaguely recognized, and the subject was
"Congratulations!"

Ariana smiled and clicked it open.

Dear Miss Covington,

I'm writing to congratulate you on your unexpected but much-deserved ascendency to the highest position in Stone and Grave. I've heard through our efficient grapevine that Princeton University is your school of choice. As a valued and high-ranking member of the Princeton Alumni Association, I'm writing to let you know that I'd be happy to help you along in the interview and application process and write you a letter of recommendation when the time comes. Feel free to contact me at any time.

Sincerely,
Geralyn Montrose, ESQ
Atherton-Pryce Hall Alumna
Princeton Alumna

"What is it?" Maria asked, munching on a single crouton. "You look like you just got excused from finals."

"Did you?" Tahira asked, quite seriously.

"No. But it's just as good," Ariana said, tucking her phone away. "It looks like I'll have no trouble getting into Princeton now, thanks to S and G."

"Was there ever any doubt?" Soomie asked, spearing a cucumber with her fork. "You've got one of the highest GPAs in our class."

Ariana lifted her shoulders modestly. "Every little bit helps, right?" She held back a laugh and smoothed her hands over her napkin in her lap. "But enough about me. This is Soomie's night."

"So where have you been all this time, anyway?" Tahira asked Soomie. "Loony bin?"

"Tahira!" Maria scolded.

Soomie laughed. "No, actually. I was at a spa in Antigua with my mom. And guys? We totally have to go back there together. That place was heaven."

As Maria and Tahira peppered Soomie with questions about her vacation, Ariana surreptitiously read Geralyn Montrose's e-mail again, keeping the phone under the table. Her giddiness nearly overwhelmed her. She was going to go to Princeton. She was going to graduate and go to Princeton and have the life she'd always wanted. The life she deserved. All she had to do was get rid of Meloni, and everything would be back on track.

LAST MEAL

"You do realize my birthday is *tomorrow*," Ariana said as Jasper led her, blindfolded, through a door and into a quiet room. From the sounds she had heard on their way here, she was pretty sure they were in a hotel—the lobby noise, the soft elevator *ping*, and the click of the electronic key had given it away—and she wondered if any of the patrons downstairs had alerted the police to her predicament. Of course, if she'd really been in the process of being kidnapped, she probably wouldn't have been giggling all the way across the lobby.

"I realize," Jasper said in her ear.

"And you also realize that one of these days you're going to have to stop blindfolding me," she joked.

Jasper ran his hands lightly over her shoulders, pushing her coat off and onto the floor. Ariana's breath caught as the mink grazed her ankles.

"Oh. But it's so much fun," Jasper whispered, sending shivers all down her back as he lightly kissed her neck.

He turned her around and walked her a few more paces into the room, then whipped the blindfold off. It took a couple of seconds for Ariana's eyes to focus, but when they did, her breath was truly taken away. In front of her was a huge, bay window looking out over Capitol Hill. The dome of the Capitol building shone in the distance, illuminated like a bright white beacon. But the view wasn't the only spectacular sight. Arranged in front of the window was a small dining table with a linen tablecloth and several silver plates, covered by crystal domes. The scents of garlic and rosemary filled Ariana's senses, and she saw a basket of southern biscuits arranged at the center of it all.

"How did you—?"

"My mother told me how much you missed your mother's cooking," Jasper said. "I know this isn't exactly the same, but . . ."

"Jasper," she said, turning to face him. "This is amazing."

"Happy birthday," Jasper replied, leaning in for a long, lingering kiss.

Ariana smiled, her lips buzzing. She couldn't have asked for a more perfect night. There was no place in the world she would rather be than here with Jasper. But as he reached for her hands, her heart pounded suddenly with the unknown. Come Saturday, she was going to start putting her plans into action. After all was said and done, she would be safe from discovery, safe from Meloni, safe from everything. Unless something went wrong. If something went wrong . . .

She couldn't even think of the alternative without shuddering.

"Are you cold?" Jasper asked, reaching his arms around her.

She shook her head and looked down, suddenly overwhelmed, afraid her voice might crack if she tried to speak. She simply couldn't bear the thought of having to say good-bye to Jasper.

Ariana took in a long breath and blew it out through her mouth. "I'm fine, really. It's just . . . you didn't have to do all this."

"Of course I did," he said simply, lifting his shoulders. "I love you."

Ariana swallowed hard and looked intently into his eyes. "How much?"

Jasper blinked, taken aback, but smiled. "I'd do anything for you. You know that."

"Anything?" Ariana asked.

He adjusted his arms on her waist, drawing her even closer. His forehead pressed against hers. Their noses touched. She could smell the mint on his breath.

"I'd go to the ends of the earth for you, Briana Leigh Covington."

Ariana's heart expanded with warmth. Her smile widened, even as the tears threatened to overflow. He couldn't have said anything more perfect. She tilted her head and touched her lips to his, gently at first. But she soon found she couldn't control her emotions and she began to press harder and harder, holding onto him as tightly as she could. Hoping she'd never have to let go.

Jasper's hand moved up her back and into her hair, cupping the back of her head. She shoved his jacket back from his shoulders and he shook it to the ground, edging her backward toward the bed. Never letting her lips leave his, Ariana tumbled onto her back, tugging him with her, and kicked her sling-back heels onto the floor. Jasper unzipped her dress, she unbuttoned his shirt, he slid his hands up under her skirt, she grasped at his bare waistline with hungry fingers.

"Wait," Jasper said suddenly, breaking away.

"What?" Ariana gasped. Her lips were swollen and her very skin throbbed. "You don't want to stop, do you?"

"No, I just . . . your food. It's gonna get cold," he said, his brow creased.

"Screw the food," Ariana replied.

Jasper grinned and she pulled his bare chest against hers, letting go of everything—of Meloni, of Reed, of the future—and giving herself entirely to Jasper Montgomery.

HAPPY BIRTHDAY

"Wait until you see inside!" Maria gushed, practically dragging Ariana and Jasper toward the double doors of the club Tahira had rented out for the birthday celebration. "We've completely outdone ourselves."

Ariana shivered with anticipation inside her white cashmere coat as Jasper squeezed her hand. She could hear the bass line of the music pounding from inside, and a screech of excitement wafted through the cold night air. For a moment, she paused at the threshold, letting Jasper reach for the door. This was it. The beginning of the biggest night of her life. She looked around, taking in the starry night sky, the twinkling lights decorating the topiary trees on the slate patio, the crisp scent of pine that hung in the air, and just like that she knew.

This was going to be a good night.

"Mademoiselle?" Jasper said, arching his eyebrows and gesturing politely at the open door. "Your celebration awaits."

Ariana grinned and stepped inside. Past a coat check and a pair of thick velvet curtains, the cavernous club opened up before them. Ariana's breath was completely taken away. Every single surface was covered with mirrors and clear crystals of all shapes and sizes. They glittered on the walls and hung from the ceiling in strands and swaths. The cocktail tables along the periphery of the hall were adorned with silver tablecloths and the centerpieces were filled with sparkling jewels. Hundreds of people crowded the dance floor, holding their champagne glasses aloft, reveling in the sheer decadence of it all.

"Happy birthday, Ana!" Soomie called out, running over and throwing her arms around Ariana's neck. She wore a dark gray full-skirted dress and black heels and looked relaxed and happy as she pulled away. "Wow. You look all . . . glowy tonight."

"I *feel* glowy," Ariana replied with a laugh. And she did. Tonight nothing and no one could touch her. Tonight, she was the star.

"Do you love it?" Tahira asked, appearing at Ariana's other side. While Soomie's dress was elegant, Tahira's was more MTV Video Awards red carpet. She wore a short, low-cut silver dress and the highest heels Ariana had ever seen, the toes encrusted with diamonds. "The theme is On the Rocks," Tahira announced, spreading her fingers wide.

"I *love* it!" Ariana exclaimed. "It's like partying *inside* a diamond."

Jasper slipped her coat from her shoulders, exposing the chic, aqua-blue sheath underneath. Maria took off her own mink jacket as well, to reveal a halter-necked black dress that just skimmed her knees and made her look impossibly slim. Jasper, gentleman that he was, hurried off over to the coat check desk with both girls' coats and bags.

"That was the idea!" Tahira cried, her eyes wide. "Happy birthday, Ana!" She gripped Ariana into a tight hug and gave her two huge air kisses.

"Thank you *so* much, Tahira. And you, too, Maria," Ariana said, reaching for Maria's hand. "This is like a dream come true."

"I'm sorry I wasn't here to help plan it, but clearly they didn't need me," Soomie said.

"I'm just glad you're here tonight," Ariana assured her. "I couldn't have asked for a better gift."

Soomie smiled, but Tahira scoffed. "Yeah, wait until you see the gift table," Tahira said, leaning toward her ear. "You'll be singing a different tune."

"Really?" Ariana asked, her eyes bright as she imagined piles and piles of elegantly wrapped presents, all with her name on them.

Thank you, Briana Leigh, for being born in December, Ariana thought happily. This party was exactly the kind of distraction she needed and the kind of celebration she knew she deserved.

"Well? Are you ready to greet your public?" Jasper asked, rubbing his hands together as he returned to her side. His sharply cut black suit fit him perfectly, and the light blue tie made his eyes seem even bluer than usual. He'd combed his hair back from his face and looked elegant and sophisticated—the perfect date for the perfect night.

"So ready," Ariana replied.

Maria pushed her long brown hair behind her shoulders. "Then let's do this, birthday girl."

Ariana grinned, and walked with her friends into the main hall.

"So let me tell you what the deal is," Maria offered, hooking her arm around Ariana's. She escorted her further into the room, where a few of Ariana's friends from school shouted their greetings and called out, "Happy birthday!"

"Clearly, this is the dance floor, but we have the upstairs lounge as well if you want to escape the mayhem for a few minutes." Maria pointed toward two sets of stairs at the back of the room, winding up in opposite directions toward a gallery area above. "Then, outside, we have the entire outdoor deck, which overlooks the water." She moved swiftly to the outskirts of the dance floor, trailing Soomie, Tahira, and Jasper toward a glass wall with several clear doors closed to keep out the cold. "As you can see, there's a hot tub out there. We're already taking bets on who'll get drunk enough to be the first skinny-dipper."

"Bet on me!" Tahira shouted, raising her arm. "I don't even need to be drunk."

Ariana cracked up laughing. "Thanks for the warning."

"This party gets better and better," Jasper joked.

"And just *wait* until you see your birthday cake!" Soomie exclaimed, raising all ten fingers. "It's incredible."

"I can't wait," Ariana replied.

"So? What do you want to do first?" Jasper asked, slipping his arm around her waist.

Ariana scanned the room, taking it all in—the happy faces, the gyrating bodies, the winking lights, the sparkling crystals. She felt so giddy she could have burst open like a bottle of Taittinger.

"Suddenly all I want to do is dance," she said with a grin.

"Woo-hoo!" Tahira cheered, throwing her arms over her head.

Jasper took Ariana's hand as the others laughed. "Your wish is my command."

After diving into the crowd, Ariana found that getting to the center of the dance floor was easy as pie. Everyone moved out of the way of the guest of honor and her entourage, and before long, she was moving to the beat with her best friends and boyfriend around her. Soon, Adam, Landon, and Rob had joined them, and Ariana smiled wider each time her entourage grew. She could feel the eyes of the crowd on her, and never before had she felt so entitled to the attention. Everything was as it should be. This was her night. She was the hottest girl at one of the most prestigious schools in the world. Everyone knew her name. Everyone wanted to be near her.

Life was perfect.

Then, she opened her eyes. And the entire world stopped spinning. There, right there, standing at the top of the dance floor scanning the crowd, was Dr. Victor Meloni in the flesh. Ariana froze and took one of Tahira's wayward elbows to the side.

"Ow!" Ariana blurted, louder than strictly necessary. She grabbed Tahira's wrist and yanked her away from the others, fighting the crowd to get to the gift table—which *was* rather impressively stocked. She ducked behind a huge Kate Spade box and pressed her back against the wall.

"I'm sorry! God! What's the matter?" Tahira hissed.

"What is *he* doing here?" Ariana asked, standing on her toes to see over the pile of presents. Meloni was moving slowly around the periphery of the room now, studying all the faces of the people on the dance floor.

Tahira whirled around, saw Meloni, and screwed her face up in confused disgust. "I have no idea," she said. "Kind of pathetic though, no? Him crashing? There aren't even any other adults here."

"Tahira, focus!" Ariana said through her teeth. "How could he have even known about this?"

Tahira lifted her shoulders and let them drop dramatically. "I don't know! I might have said something in our therapy session about planning your party for you—you know, dealing with my grief by throwing myself into a project. He seemed impressed, actually. I—"

Ariana groaned and gripped her forearm tightly. She curled her fingers and squeezed, trying as hard as she could to keep it together.

"What's the big deal? Do you want me to ask him to leave?" Tahira said, turning to the side. "Because what the birthday girl wants, the birthday girl gets!"

For a split second Ariana almost agreed to the plan. Let Tahira be the bouncer. But then she realized it was pointless. Dr. Meloni was here because he knew he would be guaranteed to finally get a glimpse of the elusive Briana Leigh Covington, and he wasn't going to leave until he got one—and probably cornered her afterward.

"No. It's okay," Ariana said. Across the dance floor, someone had stopped Meloni to talk, and he now had his back to her. "I'm just going to run to the bathroom to freshen up and maybe say hello to a few people. I'll be back."

"Okay," Tahira said. She shrugged once more, than shoved her way back into the throng of dancers.

Ariana took a moment to herself to breathe.

Shit, she thought. *Shit, shit, shit.*

This was not the way this was supposed to play out. She was supposed to have more time. She had a whole plan, which she'd yet to execute. Ariana narrowed her eyes as Meloni broke away from his conversation and resumed his deliberate search of the party.

"Screw it," she said under her breath. "I can do this."

Then she turned and took the darkest, most camouflaged route to the coat check, where she retrieved her bag and coat. She shoved her way outside and handed her ticket to the valet.

"Wait. My car's right there," she said, spotting the Porsche. "Just give me the keys."

The fresh-faced valet hesitated. "But I'm not supposed to—"

"Just *give me the keys*!" Ariana demanded.

He handed her the keys, his hand shaking. Ariana stormed over to her car, angrier about having to leave her party than anything else. As soon as she was safely inside behind the wheel, the engine started, she took out her phone and dialed Dr. Meloni's cell phone number.

It took a few rings for him to answer, and when he did, the first thing she heard was the music. Dr. Meloni was at her birthday party right now and she wasn't. How entirely wrong was that?

"Hello?"

Ariana took a breath and closed her eyes. "Dr. Meloni?" she said, pitching her voice up and throwing in a Texan accent. "Is this Dr. Meloni?"

"Yes it is." The background noise grew duller now. He was moving away from the dance floor. "To whom am I speaking?"

"Dr. Meloni, this is Briana Leigh Covington," Ariana said, infusing her voice with emotion, choking herself up.

"Miss Covington! I'm at your birthday party right now. Where are you?" he said.

Ariana clenched her jaw for a moment before answering. "I . . . I couldn't do it. I couldn't face all those people. Not tonight. I need someone to talk to, doctor. Immediately. Tonight."

"Of course!" He sounded happy, the jackass. Elated, actually. Because he'd won. He'd turned out to be right. Ariana's fingernails dug into the skin on her thigh.

"Can we meet somewhere private? Somewhere away from campus? I can't be here anymore. There are just too many memories. Too many ghosts," Ariana said, sounding tearful.

"Of course, of course. We can meet at my house. I'll give you directions."

There was dead silence behind his voice now. He was probably getting his coat.

"I have GPS," she said flatly. "Just give me the address."

He did, and Ariana stared at the front door of the club. It wasn't like she needed to write it down. She'd long since memorized the route. Seconds later, Meloni strode out the front door and handed his ticket to the valet.

"I'll be there in half an hour," she said, glaring at him through the side window of her Porsche.

"Good. And Miss Covington? I'm glad you called," he said.

I'll bet you are, Ariana thought.

"Me too," she said with some effort. Then she ended the call.

The valet pulled the doctor's car around. He hoisted himself up behind the wheel and slammed the door, a Cheshire grin on his face. Ariana wished she could have walked over to him right then and there and shot him directly through the front of his skull. But she had no gun, and there were way too many people around anyway.

Ariana scrunched down in her seat, waiting for Dr. Meloni to drive on by. As his SUV roared past her rear bumper, she envisioned herself slamming her car into reverse and taking him out. She wanted to drive her fist through the windshield, yank his lifeless body out through the shattered glass, throw him to the asphalt, and run over him multiple times with his own car, reveling in the crack of each and every bone, the squishing and splurting of his vital organs, the lakes and rivers of blood. But since she was not a possessor of superhuman strength, and since that dream was unrealistic, she decided to just breathe.

In, one . . . two . . . three . . .

Out, one . . . two . . . three . . .

In, one . . . two . . . three . . .

Out, one . . . two . . . three . . .

Instead, she took comfort in knowing that at least the very clueless Dr. Meloni was headed toward his death, and in approximately one hour, she'd be headed back to her party.

EVIDENCE

In the yard behind Dr. Meloni's house Rambo barked his fool head off, every high-pitched yelp like a pinprick to Ariana's nerves. She stood in front of the fourth window on the side of the house, saying a silent prayer that this one would give unlike the first three, then she pressed her fingers into the glass and shoved upward. The window slid noiselessly open. Ariana smiled. Finally. She was in.

She hoisted herself through the window and carefully lowered her feet onto the floor of what appeared to be a guest bedroom. Slowly, she crept to the doorway and listened. Meloni's voice. He was already on the phone. She had given him ten minutes to get settled before getting out of her car and creeping around the house, but of course he couldn't just wait for her. The man always had to be doing something, anything, to make himself feel important. Ariana peeked her head around the corner and saw that at the very end of a long hallway, a door stood slightly ajar, soft yellow light pouring out from inside.

Ariana took a deep breath and steeled herself. This was it. The moment of truth.

She tiptoed to the end of the hall and hovered right outside the doorway, relishing the moment. Maybe this wasn't the way this was supposed to happen, but it *was* happening. She might as well let herself enjoy it. Dr. Meloni was so deliciously oblivious. He had no idea she was here. He had no idea what was about to happen.

"But that's exactly why you need to take some time to think," Dr. Meloni said urgently on the other side of the thick, oak door. "There's no reason good enough to consider taking your own life."

Ariana gritted her teeth and rolled her eyes closed. He was on the phone with a patient. And this was just like him, trying to tell people what were good reasons and what were bad reasons—acting like he knew everything about everything and it was all so black and white. What did he really know about the person on the other end of that line? Ariana's fingers curled inside her black leather gloves.

In fifteen minutes, you'll be on your way back to your friends, to Jasper, to your party and your life, Ariana told herself, taking long, soothing breaths. *Just get through this and all will be well.*

Dr. Meloni hung up the phone and heaved a sigh. Ariana's pulse sped up to an alarming pace, but suddenly, she saw everything around her more clearly. Just like that, her adrenaline brought focus. She pressed her lips together and pushed the door wide. She didn't even try to conceal her face.

Dr. Meloni looked up from his desk with a start. His jaw fell open and his eyes widened in shock. All the blood drained right out of his face, from his temples to his cheeks to his chin. Even with her new hair, and even though she was supposed to be dead, he clearly recognized her.

"You," he croaked.

Ariana took a step into the room and smiled.

"Miss me?"

The doctor reached for his phone. Ariana leaped forward, tore the reading lamp from the corner of his desk, knocking over a cup full of pens and pencils, and swung as hard as he could. The heavy metal base cracked across his jaw, sending a spurt of blood over the wall where it showered his precious framed degrees—arranged just as they'd been in his office at the Brenda T.—with thick red spots. The phone slipped from his hand and he went down, slamming his chin into the edge of the desk. His head whipped back and she heard the telltale crack of his spine breaking. As his heavy body slumped to the floor, his eyes rolled into his skull. At first, one arm crooked over the arm of his leather chair, but then, ever so slowly, it slipped off and landed on the hardwood with a thud.

Her chest heaving, Ariana slowly walked around the end of the desk. Dr. Meloni was curled up at an unnatural angle, blood seeping from his mouth onto the floor. She tossed the lamp and caught it by its neck, then crouched over his feet, letting out an amused, derisive snort.

"That was almost anticlimactic," she said with a sneer.

Suddenly the doctor's eyes popped open. He grabbed a gold letter opener off the floor, let out a wet, guttural growl, and swung. Ariana felt the stabbing pain in her side before she even registered the fact that he'd moved. She shouted out, raised the lamp over her head with both hands, and brought it down with all her body weight on the front of Dr. Meloni's skull. Instantly, he fell back again. When Ariana shakily lifted the lamp, the entire front of his head was crushed inward. There was blood everywhere, and he was gone. Truly and utterly gone.

Ariana tried to breathe, but her lungs caught over and over again. She put her gloved hand over her wound and it came back covered in blood. She was supposed to do this without leaving any evidence, but now . . . now there was no way to be certain that some of the blood on the floor wasn't hers.

Her eyes filled with hot, angry tears as she looked around shakily, trying to decide what to do. She caught a glimpse of the gold letter opener, glinting in the overhead lights. It was soaked in her blood. When she reached out to grab it, she felt her wound open further and she winced. A few drops of blood slipped from her dress and hit the floor.

"Oh, God. Oh God, oh God, oh God," Ariana wept. She shoved the letter opener into her coat pocket and used her sleeve to try to wipe up the droplets. She only succeeded in smearing them into the grainy wood planks.

"This isn't happening," Ariana whispered hoarsely. "This is *not* happening."

Reaching up to clutch the desktop, Ariana dragged herself up to standing. The pain in her side was excruciating, and she was starting to wonder if Meloni hadn't hit a major organ. She fought for breath and tried to think. What did this mean? What did she need to do?

Think, Ariana. Just think.

When the police arrived, as they would eventually, they wouldn't find any fingerprints, but they would find blood. When they tested the blood, they would not be able to identify it as Briana Leigh Covington's, but they would be able to match it with Ariana Osgood's criminal file. This would, of course, stump them for a time. Ariana was supposed to be dead. But DNA didn't lie and eventually they would figure out that Ariana had faked her own death. They would figure out that she had assumed a new identity. They would put her picture everywhere. They would come looking for her, and as Meloni was currently employed at Atherton-Pryce Hall, that would certainly be their first stop.

She had to get out of here. As soon as possible. She had to get the hell out of Washington, out of the United States.

It was time to haul ass.

Taking a few tentative steps toward the door, Ariana found she couldn't move much without pain. She grabbed Meloni's scarf from a hook by the door and pressed it against the wound, staunching the blood flow. It helped her move a bit more freely, too, and she was able to nudge the door open with her foot. She opened the Internet connection on her cell phone and toggled directly to the page for Intercontinental Air. Ariana had already booked tickets for Emma Walsh and Jasper Montgomery on a three a.m. flight to Portugal, plus a nice but not ostentatious hotel room in Lisbon. All she had to do was hit CONFIRM.

Standing in the hallway, Ariana's eyes caught on a stack of mail resting atop a small table. The top envelope bore the Atherton-Pryce

Hall crest. Her heart squeezed so tightly she staggered sideways, and had to brace herself on the far wall. Suddenly, the last few months seemed like a dream. Scoring a spot at the prestigious school. Making all these amazing friends. Winning the Welcome Week competition and moving into Privilege House. Being with the most coveted guy on campus. Masterminding her pledge class plot to score points with her secret society. Getting elected president of Stone and Grave. Falling in love with Jasper. Being offered a guaranteed admission to Princeton. It had been everything she ever wanted. And now, she had to let every bit of it go.

Every bit of it except Jasper, she reminded herself as she started down the hallway, her legs quaking beneath her. *You may have to give up the future you always wanted, but at least with Jasper, you'll have some kind of future.*

She made it through the front door and out into the cold, where Rambo's bark still split the air. Cursing Dr. Meloni under her breath for the last time, she limped her way across the driveway as fast as she could go.

A PROMISE

Ariana slammed on the brakes of her silver Porsche outside the club and one of the valets jumped to open her door. She pushed herself up and out, still holding Meloni's scarf to her side underneath her coat. As she tried to stand up straight, a lightning bolt of pain shot through her abdomen, and she found herself unequal to the task. She leaned hard on the door, practically doubled over, and tried to look as if she was simply relaxing.

"Good evening, Miss," the valet said with a smile, holding the car door for her.

"I don't want you to park it," she said, a bead of sweat slipping from her temple down her cheek. She folded her coat over her dress, the skimpy fabric of which was completely soaked through with blood. The pain was growing unbearable. She had to get Jasper and get him to take care of her, or she was going to end up in a hospital, which would be the worst possible thing. "I need you to do me a favor."

"Oookay," the guy said, clearly confused.

She pulled her phone out and brought up a picture of Jasper. "See this guy?"

He nodded.

"Good. Go inside and get him for me," Ariana ordered. Then she fell back into the leather bucket seat.

The valet hesitated. "Um . . . I'm not really supposed to leave my station."

Ariana tugged a crisp hundred-dollar bill out of her wallet and handed it to him. His eyes widened in disbelief. "Go."

"Yes, Miss."

He ran inside, letting the door slam behind him. Ariana leaned back in her seat, the exhaust making steam clouds against the night air, and closed her eyes. She imagined all of her friends inside, dancing, eating, drinking, wondering where she'd gone off to, assuming she was in another part of the club. She imagined how confused they'd be when they finally realized she'd ditched her own party, how devastated they'd be when they realized she was gone from APH entirely. She hadn't decided yet whether or not to leave them a note. Certainly it would be the kind thing to do—to tell them she'd simply decided to drop out and move to Europe. It would keep them from fretting that she was dead, and probably keep Soomie out of the loony bin. But would it help or hurt her cause with the police? Part of her thought it would help because if she simply disappeared, they would be suspicious of her. But part of her thought it would hurt because it would let them know her plan.

Perhaps she could tell them she was going to Australia or Hawaii or Africa. Throw them off for a little while at least.

"Ana?"

Ariana's eyes popped open at the sound of Jasper's voice. He hovered next to her door, his cheeks ruddy with the cold. She'd never seen anything so perfect before in her life.

"Hey," she said weakly.

Jasper crouched next to the open door. "Are you all right? You look sick."

"I'm—"

Ariana shifted and the scarf tumbled out from under her dress, caked with blood.

"Holy—Ana! You're hurt!" he whispered harshly.

"It's not as bad as it looks," she told him, pushing herself up straight.

"We have to get you to a hospital." Jasper fumbled for his phone.

"No." She gripped his wrist so tightly he froze. "Jasper, no. Do you remember, last night? What you said to me?"

Jasper's brow knit. "What I said . . . ?"

"About going to the ends of the earth for me?" Ariana prompted.

His eyes registered perfect clarity. "Of course."

"Well I have to go. I have to leave the country. Now. Tonight," she said furtively. "I came here to ask . . . will you come with me?"

Jasper leaned back on his heels. "Are you . . . you can't be serious."

Ariana felt his words inside her heart like a thousand tiny daggers. "Dead serious." She reached for his hand and squeezed.

"Jasper . . . please. I need an answer. Are you coming with me or not? I have a hotel room in Lisbon. We could be there first thing tomorrow. We could start a new life. One where no one knows me . . . knows us."

Ariana realized she was rambling and bit down hard on her bottom lip.

"So. Will you come?"

"Okay, you're freaking me out here," Jasper said. "Just tell me what's going on."

Ariana's mouth hardened into a thin line. Jasper almost never spoke so colloquially. "You're stalling."

His eyes widened. "What? No? I just . . . you're bleeding and you're talking about leaving the country like some kind of fugitive and I'm not sure you're thinking straight. Let me get you some help and we'll—"

He started to get up, but Ariana grasped his hand and pulled him back down again.

"Jasper, there's no time." She looked him dead in the eye. "I know this a lot to ask, but I also know that you love me. And because I love you, I'm going to give you some time to think about it. Just . . . not too much."

She let him go and he stood up, backing up enough for her to slam the car door closed. Her finger trembled as she pressed the button to lower the window.

"If you want to be with me, meet me at Terminal A at Ronald Reagan International in four hours. And bring your passport."

"Ana . . . please. Let's talk about this," Jasper said, his nose turning red with the cold. "Tell me what's happening."

"I don't have the time, Jasper," she said, shaking her head, trying to keep the tears from spilling over. "You're going to have to decide this on your own. And please, just . . . don't tell anyone you saw me out here."

Then she closed the window, shoved the car into gear, and pulled away. She gave Jasper one last look in the rearview mirror as she reached the edge of the parking lot. The sudden pain in her heart nearly choked her. This couldn't be the last time she'd ever see him. She couldn't handle the idea that this was the end.

Come with me, Jasper, please, she thought desperately. *I don't want to lose you, too.*

ALMOST EVERYTHING

Ariana gritted her teeth as she cleaned the blood around her wound with antiseptic wipes. Every time the medicated cloth came within as much as a centimeter of the cut, the pain was excruciating. The countertop around the sink in her private bathroom was littered with crumbled, red scraps. Her chest heaving as she tried to breathe, Ariana finished the job and looked in the mirror. The gash wasn't as deep as she'd originally thought. The bleeding had slowed considerably, and even though it hurt like nothing she'd ever experienced before, she was reasonably certain she would live.

She reached for the gauze and tape she'd swiped from the emergency kit in the hallway. Gritting her teeth, she covered the wound with a large piece of gauze and taped it down tightly. Then she used an ACE bandage to wrap her abdomen and keep it from moving too much when she walked. When she was finally finished, Ariana took a few test steps around the bathroom. The cut still stung and her side ached, but it was nothing like it had been. This, she could deal with. This would not slow her down.

Ariana swiped all of the messy gauze and wipes and bandages into a small garbage bag where she'd already stashed her ruined dress and Meloni's blood-caked scarf. Then she took out two antiseptic cleaning wipes and carefully, meticulously, rubbed down every last inch of the sink, the counter, the mirror, and the floor in front of the vanity. She added these to the garbage bag and tied it tight. Later, she would dispose of the bag in a Dumpster at the airport, where it would be whisked away before anyone even knew she was gone.

Back in her room, Ariana threw on a soft black turtleneck sweater and tossed the first aid equipment into her Louis Vuitton satchel, the one she intended to carry onto the plane. Already stashed inside were her Emma Walsh passport and wallet, two thousand dollars in cash, her laptop, a change of clothes, and plenty of reading material. Her Louis Vuitton rolling trunk was full of winter clothes and coats.

Ariana snapped the trunk closed and looked around her room. Her eyes fell on the stack of opened and unopened invitations on her desk, and her heart gave a pang. The Princeton catalog lay at the center of the workspace, looking glossy and colorful and inviting. On the shelf above her bed was the framed photograph of her, Lexa, Maria, Soomie, and Brigit taken at the fund-raiser back in September—the one frame she had managed not to shatter after Meloni had shown up on campus. On impulse, Ariana grabbed the picture, shoved it into her carry-on, and zipped it closed. She took a deep breath and resolved not to cry, not to wonder what if, not to regret. Right now, she had to be practical. She had to make sure she hadn't left anything behind for the police to find. Everything seemed to be in order, and it had taken her less then twenty minutes to pack.

"Well. This is it. Good-bye, Briana Leigh Covington," Ariana said, making sure to keep her voice steady.

Then she righted her rolling trunk, slid out the handle until it clicked, and walked out the door.

STALKING HER PREY

Ariana stood in the Georgetown library while Reed participated in an American lit study group, safely hidden behind a huge shelf full of dusty sociology books. Her situation, she realized, was far from ideal. She had spent the last two weeks of her life stalking and studying and planning for this and now, she'd been forced to work off the cuff. But at least she had spotted Reed leaving for the library the moment she'd arrived. That had been a stroke of luck. Of course, it would have been more convenient had she been alone, but beggars couldn't be choosers. She would simply have to stand here and wait. Wait until this ridiculously long, Friday night discussion of Toni Morrison's life work was finally over.

This girl really did have no life.

At least it was warm inside the library. And the pain beneath her hastily applied gauze was nothing but a dull ache now. For the moment, Ariana chose to look at the bright side.

"All right, tomorrow afternoon we'll go over *Sula* and *Jazz*," the scruffy dude who'd been popping his gum all night said, closing his laptop. "Thanks, everyone, for coming on such short notice."

Ariana's chest flooded with relief and excitement as Reed began to pack up her things. The two other girls in her group—the ones she had walked to the library with earlier—said good night and strolled off together, while Reed and the scruffy dude made for the door. Ariana waited until they were nearly to the checkout desk before emerging from between the stacks. She hovered near the bulletin board while they adjusted their scarves and gloves, said their good-byes, and went outside. Then, heart pounding, she quickly followed. At the top of the steps, she paused. Scruffy dude had headed off to the right. Reed was walking in the opposite direction, toward her dorm, and she was alone.

Thank you, thank you, thank you, Ariana thought, practically skipping down the steps. She made sure to stay a good fifty paces behind Reed as she navigated the frosty, ice patch–dotted pathway toward her dorm.

Please just let her be going home. Don't let her stop anywhere along the way, Ariana begged silently. She couldn't take the suspense much longer. She needed to get this over with and get to the airport ASAP. If Reed managed to stall for very long, there was a good chance Ariana was going to have to abort her mission and go—that she was going to have to leave Reed alive.

The very thought made bile rise up in the back of her throat. The girl had to die. She simply had to die.

Ariana held her breath as Reed made the left and hurried toward her dorm, her head bowed against the frigid wind. She waited, feeling giddy with anticipation, as Reed used her key to get inside. Then she stood out in the cold for a good forty-five seconds, until someone else came out and she was able to grab the door.

The elevator doors were just sliding closed. Ariana watched as the numbered lights above the door illuminated, stopping on the third floor. Then she turned toward the stairwell and ran. She took the steps sometimes two, sometimes three at a time, and burst out into the hallway on the third floor. Reed was just slipping around the far corner. Ariana hustled to catch up. It wouldn't be long now. Not long now until she had her fingers around Reed's throat. Until she was squeezing the last gasping breath from the girl's lungs.

She paused at the corner as Reed opened her dorm room door, then sprang out of hiding as it began to swing closed. With one mighty lunge, she stopped the door with her hand before it was able to click shut and lock. Pressing her lips together to keep from laughing out loud, she swung the door open and stepped into the tiny dorm room behind her prey.

Reed turned around with a smile, undoubtedly expecting to find someone she knew. The moment she saw Ariana, she turned to stone. Her lips drained of color, her coat dropped to the ground, and she screamed.

Ariana had never heard anything so lovely in her life.

OVER

Reed's eyes darted left, then right, and Ariana saw it register in her eyes. She was going to die. She knew she was going to die.

Slowly, Ariana smiled. It was so delectable, so perfect, so much more gratifying than she had ever imagined. Every single thing Ariana had been through to get here—all the death, all the pain, all the hunger, all the fear, all the loss, all the paranoia, all of it—was now worth it.

"Hello, Reed," she said, tilting her head. "Don't you have a hug for your old friend?"

"You're dead. You're supposed to be dead," Reed said, taking a step back.

Her butt bumped against her desk and she stumbled sideways. She was so scared, so thrown, so trembly—just like a baby rabbit. Ariana advanced slowly, savoring every moment. She had a feeling this was going to be too easy, and she suddenly wanted more than anything to make it last.

"Yes, well. Don't believe everything you read," Ariana said. She picked up a framed photo from atop Reed's dresser. It was a picture of Reed, Noelle, Taylor, and Kiran, taken fairly recently. "Aw." She turned it around to face Reed. "And then there were two."

Then she flung the photo at the wall and pounced. As her leather-gloved fingers closed around Reed's slim neck, Ariana felt every bit of her anger, every bit of her frustration, every bit of her venom course into her hands. She pushed her thumbs deep into Reed's clavicle and bore down, pressing as hard as she possibly could. Her teeth gritted together and her eyes felt as if they were going to burst from her skull.

"No," Reed croaked, grasping for Ariana's wrists. "Stop . . . please. . . ."

"Yes, yes, yes. Beg me," Ariana said through her teeth. "Beg me not to do it. Please, just beg me."

She let up just the tiniest bit, giving Reed room to speak.

"Please, Ariana," she whispered, holding on to her wrists. "Please . . ."

"That's it. God, you have no idea how long I've waited to hear you say that," Ariana said. Then she squeezed even harder, leaning in, slamming the back of Reed's skull against the shelf above the desk.

Reed's eyes began to unfocus. They began to slowly roll from side to side. It was all Ariana could do to keep from laughing. She had thought she wanted APH. She had thought she wanted Princeton. She had thought she wanted a career and a home and children and love. But now she realized that it was all about this. All about this moment.

All she really wanted in the entire world was to watch Reed Brennan die.

And then, something suddenly cracked against the side of her head, and Ariana's vision blackened over. Her arms dropped at her sides and she fell against the bed, then slid to the floor. Her fingers instinctively went to her skull. As her vision began to clear, she brought them in front of her face. They were covered in blood.

Reed was doubled over coughing. In her hand was a heavy white mug. Ariana could just make out the Easton Academy logo emblazoned across the side.

"What . . . how did you . . . ?" Ariana blinked and shook her head. Darts of pain jabbed into her skull, and she felt momentarily dizzy. *Can't take your eyes off her for a second,* Ariana thought as she pushed herself to her feet. It was a mistake she wouldn't repeat.

As Reed started to regain her breath and stood up straight again, Ariana focused. She shoved the girl as hard as she could with both hands, slamming her back against the desk. Reed reeled around and cracked Ariana across the cheek with her fist. Ariana's head jerked to the right, but she instantly whirled back around and landed an even harder punch against Reed's left temple. Reed fell sideways onto the bed, and Ariana didn't hesitate. She pounced on her victim, flattening her back on the bed, her knees pressed with all her weight into Reed's shoulders. Reed's hands were above her head and under her pillow, in a pathetic gesture of surrender. Ariana closed her hands around her throat once again.

This time she was not going to stop until the girl was dead.

"It's all because of you," Ariana said, pressing down. "My whole life sucks because of you."

Suddenly, Reed's knee jabbed upward, and she shoved Ariana off of her with a force Ariana wouldn't have thought possible. She caught herself on the end of the bed as Reed sat up, drawing her hands out from under her pillow. Drawing out with them a small black gun.

Ariana's eyes widened. She staggered backward, her heart pounding an erratic beat in her ears. Slowly, Reed stood up, grasping the gun with both hands like a professional, training it on Ariana's heart.

"What the . . . ?" Ariana stuttered out, staring at the gun.

"A lot's changed since you last saw me, Ariana," Reed snapped, her voice hoarse. "And just so we're clear, your whole life *sucks* because you're a sorry-ass excuse for a human being."

No. No, no, no. This was not the way this was supposed to happen. Ariana was supposed to see Reed die. She was supposed to take Reed's life. Reed Brennan had taken every last thing from her. She could *not* let her take this, too.

She must die . . . she must die . . . she must die . . .

I am in control here, Ariana thought desperately. I *am in control.*

"Now, why don't you just stay over there against the wall while I call the police?" Reed suggested haughtily, taking one hand off the gun to reach for her phone.

Ariana flinched, seeing her opportunity. She let out a screech from the bottom of her lungs that held within it every last ounce of fury she had inside of her and lunged for Reed. A shot went off, ringing in her ears, deafening her to everything else. She saw Reed staring down at her in shock and disgust as blood seeped from her chest. Then she hit the floor at Reed Brennan's feet, and everything went black.

GRADUATION

"I can't believe we're graduating tomorrow," Ariana said, cuddling deep into her boyfriend's arms. The verdant branches overhead swayed lazily in the breeze as Thomas Pearson leaned back against the oak tree's thick trunk. All across the Easton Academy quad, students lazed about, chatted on cell phones, and tipped their faces toward the early summer sun.

"I can't believe I'm sleeping with the valedictorian," Thomas replied, his blue eyes mischievous.

"Thomas!" Ariana protested, her jaw dropping in mock offense even as she grinned.

"Okay, ew," Kiran Hayes said, throwing a bit of bagel at Thomas's head. "It's too early in the morning for that visual."

"Just showing off," Thomas replied with a shrug. He nuzzled Ariana's neck and she closed her eyes, taking in a deep breath—drinking in the warm, musky smell of him.

"What else is new?" Dash McCafferty asked, nudging the back of Thomas's shoulder with his knee as he and Noelle Lange rounded the tree.

Noelle tucked her flouncy skirt beneath her as she sat on the picnic blanket laid out under the tree and lifted her thick, dark hair over her shoulder. She looked around, her expression typically irked as she reached for a bagel.

"*Where* is the coffee?" she groused. "I need coffee."

"As always, your wish is my command," Taylor Bell called out, arriving with two trays of iced drinks. She placed them down in front of Noelle and stood up straight, shaking her blond curls back from her face.

"Were you going to join us, or were you just going to hover?" Noelle asked, taking a sip of her latte.

Taylor narrowed her blue eyes. "I don't know. Something feels off today, doesn't it?"

"Off?" Ariana asked, tucking her long blond hair behind her ear as she reached for a coffee. "It's June, the sun is shining, we're all here together. This is the perfect day."

She took a sip of her coffee, then offered the straw to Thomas. He gave her a sly smile, one that sent shivers of happiness all through her body, as he leaned in and took a sip. But when he sat back again, his face looked suddenly pale. Almost gray.

"Thomas?" Ariana said, concerned. "Are you all right?"

"I don't know," he said, clearing his throat. "Does anyone else feel cold?"

"I'm freezing," Kiran replied, tugging a leather jacket around her slim shoulders.

Ariana glanced up at the bright sun, the gorgeous blue sky, but suddenly the sun seemed *too* bright, the sky far too vivid a blue, and her heart skipped a frightened beat. When she looked down again, it took a moment for her vision to clear of the floating, purple spots caused by the sun's glare. When she could finally focus again, she saw that Kiran's skin had gone waxy. She looked positively ill. Halfway dead, really.

"What the hell?" Dash said suddenly, his cheek full of unchewed bagel. "Thomas. You're bleeding."

Thomas was white as snow now. He lifted his hand to his head and his fingers came back caked with blood. A single rivulet of dark red blood seeped past his ear and dripped off his chin. "What?"

"Oh my God, Thomas!" Ariana cried, recoiling. "What happened?"

"I . . . I don't know," he stammered, his eyes full of betrayal, full of sadness. "I . . . I thought you loved me."

"But I did!" Ariana cried. "I do! I love you more than anything. I don't understand. I don't understand what's happening."

"*What* is that infernal noise?" Noelle asked, staring up at the sky.

Ariana blinked rapidly, squinting up into the now-blinding sun. A rhythmic, persistent beeping noise filled the sky, the air, the world. She blinked harder, trying to see past the light. Trying to see Thomas. She had to make sure he was okay. In less than twenty-four hours they would graduate from Easton, have their picture taken as class couple, run off to Europe together for the summer and then to Princeton in the fall. It was just as she had always dreamed. She couldn't let go of it now. She refused to let go.

And then, suddenly, she took in a painful, gasping breath and her eyes popped open wide. She wasn't at Easton at all. And she wasn't blinking at the sun. She was staring up into the intense white light of an operating lamp. And someone was squeezing her hand.

"Ana? Ana? Oh my God. You're awake!"

"Jasper?" she croaked. She tried to focus on his face, his mouth, his eyes, but everything was blurry.

"Her name's not Ana," Noelle's voice said from somewhere at the foot of the bed. "Why do you keep calling her that?"

"Noelle? Noelle! You're here," Ariana cried, a tear slipping down her temple.

"Try not to move, hon," a gruff voice ordered, shoving her shoulder down.

"Ana, I was there. I was at the airport waiting for you. I . . . I saw you on the news and came right over," Jasper rambled. "You're gonna be fine, okay? You're going to be fine."

But the grim face of the doctor hovering at the other side of the bed said otherwise. What was wrong with her? Ariana did a mental scan of her body and realized she couldn't feel a thing. No aches, no pains, nothing. Nothing but cold.

Cold, just like Thomas. Cold like Kiran. She had just been with them. They had been right here. Ariana blinked against her stinging eyes, trying to reconcile the happy, vivid memory of where she'd just been with this harsh, unrelenting reality.

"And then I tried to call the police, and that was when . . . when she lunged at me. And I just fired."

Ariana's blood curdled. Reed Brennan. That was Reed Brennan's voice. She turned her head ever so slightly and saw her, standing in the hallway just outside the room, perfectly alive and well, giving her statement to a blue-clad officer. Suddenly it all came back to Ariana in a rush. Following Reed back to her room. Strangling the life out of her. Being kicked in the gut. And the gun. Oh, God. The gun.

"Noelle?" Ariana asked. "Noelle, please, I—"

Jasper released her hand. Noelle stepped over to the bed and looked down at Ariana. Her brown hair was pulled back in a tight ponytail and her face was grim, her eyes hard. Ariana swallowed, her throat so dry she almost choked.

"She's not your friend. Look what she . . . she . . . she tried to kill me. You can't be friends with her. You can't. I'm your best friend, right? We were always . . . always . . . together. . . . Best friends forever, right?"

Noelle's eyes flicked to something or someone across the room. Her skin looked green under the lights. She pressed her lips together. Gritted her teeth. And then, she smiled.

"Of course, Ariana. You'll always be my best friend."

Ariana let out a choked sob of happiness and reached for Noelle's hand, but Noelle's fingers jerked away. Ariana blinked, but before she could ask what was wrong, a loud, long, wailing tone filled the air. Ariana felt her heart stop beating. Her chest tightened unbearably. Her vision grayed just as Reed came into the room and stood next to Noelle.

No. I won't let go, Ariana thought. *I won't. I'm in control here.* I *am in control.*

But the breath refused to come. Her heart refused to respond. The last thing she saw as she closed her eyes was Reed Brennan—her awful face, those hated brown eyes staring down at her—as Noelle Lange held her close to her side.

Dear Maria, Soomie, and Tahira,

I know this is going to come as a surprise to all of you, but I'm leaving APH. I wish that I had the time to say good-bye, but sometimes, when you make a decision like this, you have to go through with it as soon as possible, before you lose your nerve. Besides, I know that if I had tried to look you guys in the eye and explain, I never would have had the strength to leave, and I need to do this. I need to go. It's simply the best thing for me right now.

One of my biggest regrets, aside from the sad fact that I won't be hanging out with the three of you every day, is leaving Stone and Grave without a leader. That's why I'd also like to use this note as my official endorsement of Soomie Ahn as my successor. Hopefully the other members will honor my wishes and elect you, Soomie, to this position—an esteemed position that I believe whole-heartedly you deserve.

Thank you so much, Tahira and Maria, for the incredible party. I fully enjoyed it for the short time that I was there. I don't want any of you to worry about me. Where I'm going next . . . it's where I belong. And I know in my heart of hearts that I will be happy there.

All my love,
Briana Leigh Covington

ACKNOWLEDGMENTS

If someone had told me five years ago that I would write an entire series about a psychotic murderess teenager, I would never have believed it. If they'd told me how much I would end up enjoying it, I would have rolled on the floor laughing. But in the end, Ariana was one of the most inspiring, enjoyable characters to write. What that says about me, I don't even want to contemplate, but I know I'm going to miss her. Therefore I must give special thanks to those who convinced me that Ariana was, in fact, the Private character who deserved her own spin-off, and who were there with me every step of the way.

Josh Bank, Lanie Davis, and Emily Meehan, thanks for convincing me to keep Ariana around. Thanks also to Sara Shandler, Julia Maguire, and Courtney Bongiolatti for all your ideas and inspiration. And, as ever, thanks to my personal support team: my agent, Sarah Burnes, and my family and friends, especially Matt, Brady,

Mom, Erin, Wendy, Shira, and Ally. Thanks to Sharren, the one friend who read them all, and to all the other fans who rooted for Ariana and let me know about your devotion on Twitter, Facebook, and on and on. I hope you stick with me for my next crazy ride!